Right danc

Ronald stepped closer to me. "So, Elizabeth. What do you say? Shall we accompany each other to the dance formal on Saturday?"

I swallowed. It felt like there was a lump in my throat the size of a bowling ball. There was no way I wanted to go to the dance with Ronald . . . I wanted to go with Blue!

"The dance on Saturday," I said, stalling for time. I frantically searched my brain for excuses.

"You don't have a date already, do you?" Ronald asked.

"Oh—no," I stammered. I'd been hoping Blue would ask me today.

"Then we can go together," Ronald declared happily. "Right? There aren't any obstacles in our way?"

I smiled at him. "No. There aren't. And, uh, yes, okay, I'll go with you." Agh! I couldn't believe those words had just come out of my mouth.

"Excellent. We can finalize our arrangements as the week goes on, then," Ronald said, as if we'd just concluded a business deal.

My smile wavered. Had I just made the absolute wrong decision? Did I even need to ask myself that question?

Don't miss any of the books in SWEET VALLEY JUNIOR HIGH, an exciting series from Bantam Books!

#1 GET REAL
#2 ONE 2 MANY
#3 SOULMATES
#4 THE COOL CROWD
#5 BOY. FRIEND.
#6 LACEY'S CRUSH
#7 HOW TO RUIN A FRIENDSHIP
#8 CHEATING ON ANNA
#9 TOO POPULAR
#10 TWIN SWITCH
#11 GOT A PROBLEM?
#12 THIRD WHEEL
#13 THREE DAYS, TWO NIGHTS
#14 MY PERFECT GUY
#15 HANDS OFF!
#16 KEEPIN' IT REAL
#17 WHATEVER
#18 TRUE BLUE
#19 SHE LOVES ME . . . NOT
#20 WILD CHILD
#21 I'M SO OUTTA HERE
#22 WHAT YOU DON'T KNOW
#23 INVISIBLE ME
#24 CLUELESS
#25 DRAMA QUEEN
#26 NO MORE MR. NICE GUY
#27 SHE'S BACK . . .
#28 DANCE FEVER

Dance Fever

Written by
Jamie Suzanne

Created by
FRANCINE PASCAL

BANTAM BOOKS
NEW YORK • TORONTO • LONDON • SYDNEY • AUCKLAND

RL 4, 008–012

DANCE FEVER

A Bantam Book / April 2001

Sweet Valley Junior High is a trademark of Francine Pascal.
Conceived by Francine Pascal.
Cover photography by Michael Segal.

Produced by 17th Street Productions,
an Alloy Online, Inc. company.
33 West 17th Street
New York, NY 10011.

ISBN: 0-553-48730-2

Published simultaneously in the United States and Canada

Bantam Books is an imprint of Random House Children's Books, a division of Random House, Inc. BANTAM BOOKS and the rooster colophon are registered trademarks of Random House, Inc. Bantam Books, 1540 Broadway, New York, New York 10036.

PRINTED IN THE UNITED STATES OF AMERICA

OPM 0 9 8 7 6 5 4 3 2 1

To Keely Alexandra Schafer

Elizabeth

"So Damon asked me to the dance today!" My twin sister, Jessica, wiggled her hips excitedly as she set down a plate on the dining-room table Sunday night.

"That's cool, Jess. Look—you're dancing already," I told her with a laugh. "Just don't drop any plates while you practice."

Well, that made *one* of us with a date for the eighth-grade formal. But it wasn't any surprise that Damon had asked Jessica already. They had sort of been going out for a long time, almost since the beginning of the eighth grade. If he hadn't asked Jessica to the formal right away, I would have been surprised. Shocked. Not to mention outraged. (Okay, not really. But it definitely would have been strange.)

The kitchen smelled delicious. Our dad was making his Sunday-night special—meat loaf and baked potatoes. Which basically meant he'd get to sit on the sofa and watch sports while everything baked for an hour. Outside, our brother,

Steven, was helping our mom with some yard work.

"And the coolest thing isn't that he asked me; it's *how* he asked me," Jessica said, opening her eyes wide for emphasis.

I waited for a second or two, but she didn't go on. She was obviously waiting for a response.

"*Well,* how did he ask you?"

"Well," Jessica chirped, looking satisfied. "I went over to his house because we were supposed to go bike riding, but when I rang the bell, nobody answered. But the door was open, so I went in. And there was a bouquet of daisies sitting in a vase on the kitchen table, with a big rose in the middle. There was a card sticking out of it with my name on it, so I picked it up and opened it, and guess what it said."

She stopped to fiddle with the flowers in the vase on the table. The arrangement had become sort of lopsided, and she straightened it up. But I knew she was just stalling. "The suspense is killing me," I said, rolling my eyes. Jessica always needs to make everything sound ten times more dramatic and involved than it actually is.

"It said: 'To a rose among daisies: Will you go to the formal with me?' "

"Oh. That's really cute, Jess," I told her. And it really was. Jessica looked so happy whenever she talked about Damon. He was really good for her. And that made *me* happy.

But I couldn't help it. I felt this horrible, ugly surge of jealousy mixed in with my happiness. I wanted someone to ask *me* to the formal. And not just anyone. I wanted Blue Spiccoli to ask me.

It was sort of silly for me to think that way because my situation with Blue wasn't anything like Jessica's situation with Damon. Jessica and Damon had been going out for a while. Which wasn't true of me and Blue. We weren't even going out. Not yet anyway.

I mean, I knew that I liked Blue, and I was pretty sure he liked me. We always had a good time together whenever we hung out. I thought he was really cute, and I knew he thought I was okay looking, at least. So we were definitely interested in each other. But I couldn't just assume that we were going to the formal together. Could I? I *wanted* to.

Jessica went into the kitchen and started bringing out bottles of salad dressing while I put napkins at each place setting.

"So, what about you?" Jessica asked. "Did Blue ask you yet?"

"Jessica? I don't think we need any more salad dressing." There were only about seven different bottles on the table already.

Jessica stopped in the doorway, juggling four more bottles. Our parents have this really annoying habit of never finishing any of them. Okay, so maybe we contribute to the problem. "You're trying to change the subject," she said. "And I'm not going to let you."

"I am not trying to change the subject," I said. "It's just that . . . I mean, it's not like Blue is definitely going to ask me. We're not going *out* or anything."

"I guess that's a no." Jessica sighed. "Well, look, it's no big deal. Maybe he's waiting for the right time. He'll probably ask you tomorrow as soon as you get to school," she predicted. "You haven't seen him all weekend. And tomorrow's kind of a big day for asking—since the dance is next Saturday."

I opened my mouth to say I didn't care if Blue asked me or not, but there was no use trying to fool Jessica. She was the one who convinced me I liked Blue in the first place, even though I'd tried for so long to convince myself that we were only friends.

But I wasn't sure she was right about Blue wanting to go with me. And as far as waiting until tomorrow to see me? Well, he could just call me, I thought, and ask me on the phone. But maybe he had been really busy this weekend. Or maybe he didn't plan on asking me. I didn't know!

"I really hope he does ask me," I confessed. "The sooner, the better. What will I do if he doesn't?"

"Duh. You'll ask *him*," Jessica said, as if it were the most obvious thing in the world. "There's no point in sitting around waiting and hoping when you can just as well ask him to the formal. You *are* in the eighth grade, remember? And anyone in the eighth grade can invite anyone they want."

She definitely had a point. "I don't know if I could get up the nerve to ask him," I said. "Does that sound stupid?"

"It's not stupid—I'd be nervous too," Jessica said. "But what's he going to do—say no? As if! He wants to go with you, just like you want to go with him. One of you just has to do the asking. And it'll happen, Liz. Trust me."

I smiled. "If you say so."

The truth was that putting myself in Blue's shoes made me realize that asking someone to a dance wasn't as easy as it sounded. I'd be so afraid he'd turn me down. I wondered if he thought I might do the same thing.

Jessica and I went into the kitchen. I started getting water glasses out of the cupboard while she got the pitcher out of the refrigerator.

"Hey, Liz. You know how I have that dentist appointment tomorrow morning?" Jessica asked.

"You're getting a cavity filled, right?" I said.

Jessica groaned. "Don't remind me."

I shrugged. "You're the one who brought it up!"

She rubbed the side of her jaw. "It's going to be such a drag. But at least I get out of algebra, so that's something. Anyway, do you think you could hand in my homework assignment for me?"

"Sure," I said, distributing the glasses around the table. "Just give it to me tonight."

"I can't," she said as she filled them with water. "I finished it Friday during study hall, so I left it in my locker for the weekend. Would you mind getting it out?"

"No problem," I said.

"You know my combo, right?"

"You'd better write it down. Just in case I forget," I said.

"Okay. And if you happen to see any mistakes, you know, when you're walking down the hall to hand it in?" Jessica asked. "It's perfectly okay if you want to correct my answers."

"Why use *my* expertise when you have Ronald?" I joked. Ronald Rheece is Jessica's locker partner—we all have to share lockers because the school is a little overcrowded. And

Ronald's kind of a brain (well, that's a nice way of putting it). But he and Jessica aren't exactly pals.

"Like he even remembers how to do algebra," Jessica scoffed. "Didn't he take that when he was like ten years old?"

"Nine, I think," I said. "He takes calculus now."

Jessica laughed. "Hey, I've got an idea. After you pick up my homework from my locker, you're sort of on the way to Blue's locker. So keep walking, go find him, and ask him to the formal."

I didn't say anything in reply. That was taking a big risk, and I didn't feel ready.

"Elizabeth! Promise me," Jessica urged. "If Blue doesn't ask you soon, you'll ask him."

I turned to her and smiled, trying to figure out a way to get up my nerve. How could she make it sound so easy when it was the hardest thing in the world to do? "Okay," I said. "I promise."

How to Ask Elizabeth Wakefield to the Eighth-Grade Formal A Stylistic Approach

By Blue Spiccoli

(who's supposed to be writing "Stylistic Approaches in Music")

Hey, Liz. What's up? What are you doing next Saturday night? (Dumb.)

Hi, Elizabeth. Would you like to go to the formal with me? (Too formal.)

Howdy, stranger. Care to be my dance pardner? (Nerd alert!)

So if I'm there, and you're there, and we sort of like happen to be there together . . . (Obviously not.)

Dude, would you *please* say yes and make me the happiest guy in the whole eighth grade? (Gag.)

Liz? Can I talk to you for a second? About you, and me, and this dance? (No way, dude!)

You. Me. Smooth grooves. Aw yeah. (Man, this is bad.)

H, as in, *How* am I going to do this without embarrassing both of us to death?

Elizabeth

When I got off the bus on Monday morning, I felt sort of strange. It was really weird to come to school by myself, without Jessica. It didn't happen very often. But I decided that as much as I didn't like Monday mornings without my twin, coming to school *had* to be better than sitting in a dentist's chair with a drill coming at me. I shuddered just thinking about it. Poor Jess!

We transferred to Sweet Valley Junior High at the beginning of eighth grade because the district got rezoned. Let's just say it wasn't the smoothest transition ever. This school's a lot bigger than our old one. All of a sudden we had new teachers, new classmates, new friends—or not. It took a while for both of us to feel at home.

The school is a two-story, brown-brick building with small windows, and inside, the walls are painted a sort of mustard yellow. Old mustard, that is (not that nice Martha Stewart kind of mustard). And it's sort of crowded.

Elizabeth

I went to Jessica's locker first thing to grab her homework because I didn't want to forget it. Once I get to my locker, my friends Anna Wang and Salvador del Valle usually come by to find me. And once we start talking, forget it. Jessica's algebra homework would totally slip my mind.

As I walked down the hall, I looked around for Blue. Sometimes he hangs out by the water fountains on the first floor, but he wasn't there today.

I stepped up to Jessica's locker and took the tiny slip of paper with her combination written on it out of my pants pocket. I spun the wheel around and then pulled open the locker.

Ronald Rheece's half of the locker was neat and organized. Jessica's looked like it had been through a tornado recently. A big one. She had a dozen books and notebooks all piled in a heap, surrounded by extra sweaters, an extra pair of sneakers, and a crumpled nylon jacket. I sorted through it all until I pulled out two items that looked vaguely related: her algebra textbook and a green notebook that said Algebra on the front. I had just grabbed a sheet of homework with that day's date on it when I felt a tap on my shoulder.

I turned around and found myself shoulder to face with Ronald Rheece.

"Elizabeth! I *thought* it was you," he said.

"You did?" I tucked Jessica's homework sheet into my backpack.

Ronald nodded, his glasses glinting in the fluorescent lights. "I can tell you and Jessica apart because you're prettier."

"Oh." I laughed. "Right." Ronald had never said something like that to me before, and I couldn't help feeling a little flustered. Anyway, it wasn't *true*—he knew it and I knew it because Jessica and I are identical.

"Sorry if it looked like I was ransacking your locker," I told Ronald. "Jessica's coming in later today, so she asked me to grab her algebra homework and turn it in for her."

"Which you're doing because you're so nice," Ronald commented.

"Well, she'd do the same for me," I said as I stepped aside from the locker to let Ronald use it.

Ronald didn't move. He kept looking at me. I wondered if I'd knocked one of my barrettes lopsided as I rummaged through the locker.

"You're looking especially lovely this morning," Ronald commented as he gazed up at me.

"Um, thanks," I said. This was really weird. Why was he being so complimentary all of a sudden? "It's nice to see you too."

Ronald raised his eyebrows. "In that case, I have a question for you."

"Oh? Okay," I said.

"Since we're both in agreement on so many things, including how pleasant it is to see each other this morning," Ronald began.

I started to get this sinking feeling in my stomach. Where exactly was Ronald going with this? And did I want to go along?

"Perhaps it would be appropriate for us to accompany each other to the dance formal on Saturday," Ronald continued. "Don't you think that would be a wise decision?"

I couldn't move. I didn't know what to say. Ronald was staring up at me with a sort of goofy, awkward smile on his face. No wonder he was being so complimentary. He was looking for a date to the dance!

He stepped closer to me. "I know this may come as a sudden shock." He patted his button-down, striped maroon shirt. "But you know, I was walking down the hall, thinking of who I might enjoy accompanying to the formal, and when I saw you at my locker, I knew it must be fate." Ronald swallowed loudly. "So, Elizabeth. What do you say?"

I swallowed too. It felt like there was a lump in my throat the size of a bowling ball. There was no way I wanted to go to the dance with Ronald . . . I wanted to go with Blue! But I couldn't tell Ronald

I was *going* with Blue because he hadn't asked me yet. And anyway, Ronald looked so nervous, standing there adjusting his glasses. (Who knew Ronald Rheece could be nervous around girls? Not me. He usually spends more time with computers than with members of the opposite sex.) I didn't have the heart to tell him I was waiting for someone else to ask me.

"The dance on Saturday," I said, stalling for time. I frantically searched my brain for excuses. *Maybe I can tell him that I'm flat-footed and I'm not supposed to do excessive physical exercise,* I thought. Nope. Ronald knew I was on the volleyball team. *Maybe I can tell him my culture forbids dancing.* Yeah, right. *Maybe I can just tell him I have another date.*

"You don't have a date already, do you?" Ronald asked.

"Oh—no," I stammered, mentally kicking myself.

"Then we can go together," Ronald declared happily. "Right? There aren't any obstacles in our way?"

I smiled at him. "No. There aren't. And, uh, yes, okay, I'll go with you." Agh! I couldn't believe those words had just come out of my mouth.

"Excellent. We can finalize our arrangements as the week goes on, then," Ronald said, as if we'd just concluded a business deal. The bowling ball in my throat dropped into my stomach. "You know, I sort of expected you to want some time to think it over. That's what most girls would say. But you're very decisive, Elizabeth. That's one of the things I've always admired about you." Ronald smiled at me again.

My smile wavered. Maybe being so decisive wasn't a good thing. Had I just made the absolute wrong decision? Did I even need to ask myself that question?

Then another, even scarier thought occurred to me.

What was Blue going to think when he found out I was going to the dance with another guy?

Blue

"Dude, is that supposed to be an enchilada?" I asked Toby Martin at lunch on Monday.

Toby nodded. "Why?"

"Just wondering. Because if that's an enchilada, then I guess *this* is supposed to be a burrito." I stuck a fork into the gnarly, loosely wrapped flour tortilla on my plate. If I tried to pick it up, I'd have burrito all over the place. Since I was waiting around for Elizabeth and planned to ask her to the dance, I couldn't exactly risk that.

I looked around the cafeteria. Where *was* Elizabeth anyway? Lunch had started five minutes ago. It wasn't like her to be late. In fact, she was always on time, while *I* was always late. She usually gave me a hard time about it.

"Well, if that's a burrito, then I guess this is supposed to be a *real* sandwich," Salvador del Valle said as he frowned at the nearly flat slices of bread stuck together in his hand. "Funny.

They said it was supposed to be peanut butter 'n' jelly, but it tastes like bread 'n' more bread. How can they be so stingy about something as cheap as peanut butter? And jelly? I mean, the two words together define *cheap*."

Anna Wang laughed. "I don't know why you guys don't bring your lunch." She opened up a plastic container of Chinese noodles and vegetables and started to eat.

"Duh! Because that would be actual work," I said. "Something I've promised myself never to get involved in."

"Yeah," Salvador said. "Not a chance. Anyway, the Doña usually takes care of it for me. But she's been slacking recently. If only she knew how much I suffer because of it." He pretended to wipe a tear from his eye.

"Not as much as I'm suffering, man," I said. "The salsa in this thing tastes like tomato soup."

Toby laughed. "The cafeteria version of Mexican food is a little watered down—you're right."

"But what can we do? They make us go to class. We get hungry," Salvador said. Suddenly Salvador's eyes lit up like he was really on to something. "So *that's* it. School is a conspiracy to get rid of the nation's stale bread and bad recipes."

Anna held a forkful of noodles out to Salvador, giggling. "Here. I take pity on you."

"Yes!" Salvador reached for the fork.

It wasn't your typical lunch period. I was enjoying cracking jokes, but I wasn't really concentrating. Not that I don't like hanging with Salvador—we're in a band together, so we're pretty good buds. And Anna and Toby are supercool. But today I was here on a mission.

I was taking another bite of the world's sloppiest burrito when Elizabeth walked into the cafeteria.

"Hey—there's Elizabeth!" Anna pointed out.

I quickly wiped my mouth with a napkin and sat up straighter. I know, I know. Not like me at all to worry about stuff like that. But what can I say? I really liked Elizabeth. A lot.

She was wearing this cute little red sweater and jeans. Her hair was pinned back in barrettes. The outfit wasn't anything all that special, but it looked great on her. Then again, what doesn't?

I reached up to sort of try to fix my hair so I didn't look completely ridiculous. Then I cleared my throat. My mouth was suddenly very dry—it gets that way when I'm nervous. I reached for my orange juice to take a few swigs. I wasn't going to let dry mouth get in my way.

But when I looked up, it didn't matter. Elizabeth had turned around and was already on her way out of the cafeteria!

"You mean, there *was* Elizabeth," Toby

commented. He looked as surprised as I felt.

"Where's she going?" Salvador asked. He looked at me.

I shrugged. Obviously I had no idea. I wouldn't be sitting there waiting for her if I didn't think she was going to sit down and have lunch with me. I was totally shocked.

"She didn't even grab anything to eat," Anna commented.

"Maybe she doesn't feel well," Toby suggested.

"Maybe she took one look at the food and decided to go home sick," Salvador joked. "Hey, it happens to the best of us."

Toby and Anna laughed, but I just nodded absently.

Then Anna looked at me with a sympathetic smile. "She must have remembered some homework she needed to do or something like that." Was it that obvious that I was waiting to ask Elizabeth to the formal?

"Sounds like Elizabeth," I said, trying to act like it was no big deal. But why hadn't she come over to at least say hi to us—to me? Was she mad at me for something I'd done—or forgotten to do? Well, I hoped not. Because now that I'd gotten my nerve up, I was determined to ask her to the dance today. I decided to cut my lunch short and go find her.

Elizabeth

I waved to Bethel McCoy as I passed her in the hallway. "Hi, Bethel!" I called.

"Hi, Liz!" she said. "Where are—"

She didn't get to finish her question because I was practically sprinting away from the cafeteria. I knew I was being sort of rude, but I couldn't help it.

Panic will do that to a person. You get this blast of superhuman energy that comes from sheer terror. Like the terror of seeing Blue sitting with Anna, Toby, and Salvador at the lunch table. On any other day I would have been so glad to see him there. But not today!

Was he planning to ask me to the dance at lunch? Was that why he was patting his hair (which is usually just shaggy) and looking so nervous when I walked in? The thought made me smile a little. But then I felt that lump from this morning rise in my throat again. I knew I was going to have to tell Blue that I'd agreed to go to the dance with Ronald. Especially if he asked me to the dance himself. And I was going to put that off as long as I could—or at least until I figured out how to tell him in a way that wasn't insulting. Was there a way? "Oh, thanks for asking me, but I'm already going with someone. Ronald Rheece, in fact." I hoped he'd understand. I tried to tell myself that he was such a nice, easygoing, laid-back guy, he'd *have* to understand. Right?

My stomach growled with hunger as I pushed open the door to study hall. Skipping lunch wasn't the best idea. Maybe I could grab something to eat at the end of lunch period.

The door closed behind me, and I realized that study hall was almost completely full. There was only one seat left! We all had lots of tests that week, so it made sense. But the only seat left was right next to *Ronald*. Just my luck. *Should I sit there?* I wondered. *Or should I go find an empty classroom to study in?* I thought for a minute about what I should do. Which was maybe a mistake because I should have bolted right then and there.

Before I could move, Ronald turned around and saw me standing there. His face lit up, and he waved hello.

I waved back. So much for my great escape. I went over and slid into the seat at the desk next to his.

"Elizabeth, what a pleasant surprise," Ronald said in a soft voice. "How did I get so lucky twice in one day?"

I shrugged as I pulled my book out of my backpack. "We must have the same schedule," I said quietly.

"No, I think it must be fate once again. The stars are perfectly aligned," Ronald said as he gazed dreamily up at the ceiling.

I smiled faintly and opened my book to start reading. For some reason, Ronald was acting completely mushy. I didn't know where it was coming from, but I hoped it would stop—soon. I might have agreed to go to the dance with him, but I hoped he didn't think I was romantically interested in him.

I had barely read a page when I heard the crinkling of plastic wrap coming from the direction of his desk. Then this peculiar smell drifted through the air. My nose twitched as a strange mixture of onions and meat filled the air. Then my stomach twitched. What in the world was that nasty smell?

Ronald leaned across the aisle and held out half of a sandwich to me. "Hungry?"

So that's what's making me so nauseous. "Um . . . no thanks," I said as I stared at the lumpy brown bread.

Elizabeth

"Come on, it's ham and egg salad on whole wheat with onions," Ronald said. "It's delicious! It's also my favorite."

"Well, then, I could never take half of it from you, could I?" I said.

"Sure, you could," Ronald said.

"No, I really couldn't." Because it looked absolutely awful! I might be hungry, but it wasn't for that sandwich. "I mean, I ate a really big breakfast this morning, so I'm not that hungry," I told Ronald. "Really—it's okay. But thanks for offering."

He gave me a puzzled look and then shrugged. "If you insist, Elizabeth. But I really am delighted to share."

I read some more while he ate his sandwich. I was getting this really uncomfortable feeling while I tried to focus on my book, though. I could feel Ronald still looking at me. Like he didn't have anything better to do. What was with him today?

I glanced over at him, hoping that would make him realize that he was sort of, um, staring.

"Elizabeth, is something wrong?" he asked, not taking his eyes off me.

"What?" I shook my head. "No. Nothing's wrong." I tried to smile.

"Are you sure?" Ronald pressed. "Because you

know, if you wanted to discuss it, perhaps that would make you feel better."

I glanced around the room. "Everyone's trying to study, so we should probably be quiet," I whispered.

"Don't worry, we can still talk," Ronald said in a soft voice. "Please, tell me what's made you so contemplative."

So *what?*

"I feel fine," I insisted. "Really. I have a lot of homework to do, though, so I should get back to that. Don't you have a lot of studying to do too?" I glanced around the room again, hoping he'd get the point. This *was* study hall.

"Maybe I do, but that's immaterial." Ronald wiped a crumb off the corner of his mouth. "I'm concerned about you."

What? I was thinking. Since when was Ronald so interested in me? "Everything's perfectly okay."

"Yes, that's what you keep saying. But your face reflects a conflicting opinion. Which is why I think you might need an act of simple human kindness," Ronald said.

Before I could figure out what he was talking about, he got up from his desk, walked over to me, and put his arms around my shoulders to give me a hug!

"You know what, Ronald? Come to think of

it, my stomach does kind of hurt." I grabbed my backpack and book and struggled out of his grasp. I stood up and smiled politely. "I'm gonna go see the nurse. Um, er, thanks. See you later!"

I rushed out of the room and into the hallway. Guess who was walking down the hall right then? Guess who I crashed right into? Blue!

"Hey, I've been looking all over for you," he said.

"Um . . . well . . . hi," I said as I backed away from him. "I have to go, but, um, I'll talk to you later!" Thankfully, the girls' bathroom was only a few steps away. I pushed open the door and leaned against the wall, panting. It felt like I was a criminal who was running from the law.

I felt so guilty for avoiding Blue like that! I'd have to tell him about my dance date sooner or later. But I couldn't do it. Not yet.

All I could think was: Why couldn't *I* be the one who went to the dentist this morning instead of Jessica? Why did I have to be at her locker? I'd been hoping that maybe the dance would be a chance for Blue and me to start being kind of a couple. Now, instead, I had a date with Ronald, and I'd blown off Blue twice in the space of a few minutes.

Actually, it felt like I was blowing everything.

Blue

Wipeout!

The door swung shut behind Elizabeth, and I stood next to the drinking fountain, thinking: *So this is how it feels to get totally blown off by the girl of your dreams.*

Okay, so maybe I'd felt blown off before. But I hadn't been blown off by Elizabeth before. I instantly hated it.

There was no doubt about it now. First the cafeteria, now this. She was definitely avoiding me.

But why? Had I done something wrong?

I couldn't think of anything that had happened lately that would make her act like this. We were getting along great, I thought.

What was going on with Elizabeth? Why did she totally hate me all of a sudden? Was she worried that I was going to ask her to the dance? Maybe she didn't really want to go with me.

And if that was true, what did that mean about us? As in, Elizabeth and Blue, the potential couple.

Dude.

Bethel

I was stretching my calves on Monday afternoon by leaning against the chain-link fence that surrounds the track when Jameel came over to me. Jameel and I are both on the track team—in fact, that's how we met and became friends. Or whatever it is we are. Friends with potential?

Jameel was wearing his usual workout clothes: long, black shorts, a white T-shirt, and his running sneakers. It was the same thing everyone else on the track team wore, more or less. But somehow Jameel managed to make it look *better* on him. How does he do that?

"Hey, Bethel," he said as he stopped beside me.

"Hi!" I replied as I pushed the front of my foot forward to get a good, long stretch. My calves always tighten up if I don't stretch them well at the end of my workout. "What's up?" I asked.

"That was a really fast four hundred I saw you run just now," he said. "Was that a personal best?"

I shook my head. "I've run it faster before. But it was still a good time for me." I looked over at him. He was smiling, and his brown eyes sort of sparkled in the late afternoon sun.

"So do you think your extra training is helping?" Jameel asked me.

"Um, sure," I said. I'd recently started doing more long-distance runs to try to build up my endurance. I'm primarily a sprinter, but my coach thought it would be a good idea if I worked on some other events, just to keep things interesting for me. "It's definitely helping, but I don't always look forward to putting in the extra miles, you know?" I told Jameel.

He nodded. "I can relate. Extra miles and me? Not exactly a good thing. My dad tried to get me to run a ten-K with him a couple of months ago, and I could hardly finish it! I think I came in dead last in my age group. In fact, I think I was last in *every* age group."

I laughed. Jameel was so funny—it was one of the things I really liked about him. "Come on, I doubt that!"

"Nope, it's true," Jameel insisted. "They even gave me a special medal—Most Spectacular Choke Ever."

I smiled and shook my head. "Yeah, right—I'll bet."

"They did!" Jameel insisted. "You'll have to come over to my house sometime, and I'll show you. We've got it displayed on the mantel."

"Sure. Okay," I said, rolling my eyes. Truthfully, the thought of going over to Jameel's house was kind of exciting. Even though he'd been to my house before, I'd never been to his. But I wasn't sure if he was really inviting me or not, so I changed the subject. "So, how was your workout today?" I asked.

"Not bad, except I kept fouling on my long jumps," Jameel said. "I don't know what it is. Some days I just can't help it—my steps are all off, and there's nothing I can do. You know?"

I nodded. "I wish I didn't," I said. "But I've been there. Just tell yourself you're getting all your mistakes out of the way in practice. Then when the meet day comes, you won't have any left."

Jameel laughed. "I'll try that." He went to lean against the fence, and his back brushed against a large, blue plastic banner that was tied to the fence.

Don't Be a Dunce! Go to the Dance! it said in big letters. Then underneath that it said, The Annual Eighth-Grade Formal. Buy Your Tickets Today! The date and time appeared at the bottom.

Oh. This was so embarrassing. How could we

be standing in front of that giant banner? I couldn't have picked a worse place to have a conversation with Jameel. It was like the banner was telling me that I should invite him to the dance.

Because Jameel is in the seventh grade, I'd have to invite him to the formal, not the other way around. And I wanted to ask him. And then I didn't want to. I was so confused. I'd been trying to decide what to do since the date of the formal was announced. Usually I'm a lot more decisive than this!

Jameel is really fun to hang around with. He has a great sense of humor, and we never run out of things to talk about. We share an interest in sports—all kinds of sports—and we both like the same music, not to mention movies and TV shows. And he's totally cute. *And* I really like him.

But he's a year younger than me, so that makes it kind of weird. A lot of girls at Sweet Valley Junior High go out with older guys—not younger guys. Taking him to the dance would be sort of . . . unconventional, I guess you could say. Not that I usually care too much about what other people think, but still, I would feel a little awkward.

And then there was the fact that Jameel was shorter than me. I'd gone through this massive growth spurt over the past several months, and I think I was about four inches taller than him. I couldn't quite picture us dancing together without me feeling like a giant—and him feeling like a shrimp.

"So. Got any plans for next weekend?" Jameel asked.

It was like he was reading my mind. Jameel the psychic. "Well, not too many," I said, trying to evade the question. If he was looking at that banner like *I* was, he was probably thinking the same thing: *Is Bethel going to ask me to the dance or not?* "How about you?" I asked, stalling for time.

"Nothing big," Jameel said. "Which is cool. I don't always like to have plans. Sometimes it's better to just see what develops, you know?" He raised his eyebrows.

"Oh yeah," I said. "Definitely."

Unless you're supposed to be finding a date to the biggest dance of the year! And he's standing right in front of you, and for some reason you just can't ask him.

Go ahead—ask him, I tried to tell myself. *What's the big deal? He wouldn't say no.*

But I just couldn't get myself to do it.

Jameel

I stood there and watched Bethel babble about how she was supposed to help her mother with some baking project the following Sunday. I couldn't believe it. I had totally given her an opening so that she could ask me to the dance.

Got any plans for next weekend?

All she had to do was say: "Well, not yet, but I was wondering if you would go to the dance with me."

It would have been so *easy*. And I thought she wanted to ask me. We both knew that we were interested in each other. I was definitely attracted to her anyway—I loved her beautiful eyes, her flawless brown skin, her infectious smile . . . I liked everything about her. And I thought she felt the same way about me. So why was she dragging her heels on this? I was starting to think Bethel wasn't as brave and strong as she always seemed. I was starting to think that deep down, she was a real *chicken* when it came to this dating stuff.

Jameel

But what could I do about it? I couldn't ask her to the dance. She was going to have to do all the hard work herself. And if she wasn't going to do it the easy way, by asking me when I gave her an opening—and we were standing right in front of the dumb sign for the dance? Maybe I should just forget about it.

Then again, I really did want to go to the dance with her. So maybe I would have to find another way to help Bethel invite me. I just hadn't figured out how yet. It was something I'd need to work on, like my long-jump steps.

Jessica

Monday night, I was holding my new dress up against me and standing in front of the mirror. I was trying to figure out how I should do my hair for the dance. It had to be perfect. So far, everything about this formal seemed perfect, and I wanted to keep it that way.

My dress was so awesome. It was sleeveless, black, and sort of shiny, with all these different clusters of green leaves splashed onto the fabric.

Kristin Seltzer and I had actually gone shopping together for dresses after school, despite the fact that Kristin's boyfriend, Brian Rainey, hadn't asked her to the dance yet. What can we say? We were feeling sort of confident. Brian and Kristin are crazy about each other. They don't really even have to ask each other stuff like that—they just seem to have one of those relationships where they can read each other's thoughts.

Just then there was a knock at the door, and Elizabeth walked in.

I twirled around for her, showing off my new dress. "Well, what do you think?"

"Nice," Elizabeth said. I would have loved a bit more enthusiasm.

"What are you going to wear?" I asked as I put the dress back into my closet, shoving aside other hangers to make room. "What's *Blue* going to wear? Or is he just going to show up in his surf shorts?" I hadn't had a chance to talk to Elizabeth after school to find out if Blue had asked her to the dance yet. But I was sure if he hadn't, he would soon.

Elizabeth didn't say anything. When I turned around, she was sitting at my desk, with her elbows on the desk and her chin resting on her hands.

"What is it?" I asked as I stopped in front of her. "What's wrong?"

"Everything," Elizabeth muttered, tossing a pencil across my desk. She looked up at me and let out a huge sigh. "Remember how you asked me to turn in your algebra homework for you this morning?"

I nodded. "You forgot to do it." That wasn't *such* a big deal. I'd explain to Mr. Wilfred tomorrow.

Elizabeth shook her head. "No, I remembered.

So I went to your locker, and I was taking out your notebook, and guess who comes walking up."

"Blue!" I blurted out.

Elizabeth shook her head again. "Not Blue. Someone else."

"Well, *who?*" I asked. Why was she drawing it out like this? Just to torture me?

She pushed a box of paper clips around the desk. "Ronald," she mumbled.

"Ronald Rheece? So?" Ronald was my locker partner. It made sense that Elizabeth would bump into him at my locker. So what was the big deal?

"So he asked me to the dance," Elizabeth said slowly, like it took a lot of effort just to form the words.

"No way!" I squeaked. Ronald Rheece had a thing for my sister? It was news to me! The poor guy was so tightly wound, he probably burst a gasket when Elizabeth turned him down.

"Wow. So when you told him you couldn't go with him, how did he take it? What did he say? You shouldn't feel bad, Liz, I mean—"

Elizabeth cut me off. "I'm not upset about hurting his feelings, Jess. I *didn't* hurt his feelings." She paused, looking down at her hands and playing with her cuticles. "I said yes," she muttered.

Jessica

"What?" Had I heard her right? Ronald Rheece was one of the geekiest, most annoying guys in school. No to mention her going to the dance with him would mean not going with Blue. "What were you thinking? What about Blue?"

"Well, you know I want to go with Blue, but—"

"But what?" I threw up my hands. "If you want to go with Blue, why did you say yes to Ronald? You're crazy!"

"Jess, I had to accept," Elizabeth said.

I folded my arms across my stomach. "Since when does anyone *have* to accept a date? Especially when they have other plans?"

"Ronald asked if I wanted to go. And I couldn't think of a good way to say no without being mean—I didn't have a date already," Elizabeth said. She sputtered a few more things about how Ronald was being so nice, she'd feel guilty for turning him down, and it obviously meant a lot to him, etc.

In my opinion, she wasn't making *any* sense. And I wasn't going to let her get away with it.

"Elizabeth, don't you realize what's going on here?" I demanded.

"What?" she asked innocently. Like she didn't know.

"You're doing everything in your power to keep things between you and Blue from getting more serious," I told her. "Just like when you kept saying that you guys were just friends. Why don't you just give in?"

"That's not true!" Elizabeth protested as she jumped up from the desk, looking really angry at me all of a sudden. But I couldn't help it. I was frustrated. I'd spent way too much time and energy trying to get Elizabeth and surfer boy together, and now she was taking three giant steps backward. Ugh!

"Look," Elizabeth said, trying to keep her voice calm. "You were right about me liking Blue all those times, and I've already admitted that. But I really did—"

Just then the phone rang, so she didn't get to finish her sentence. I'd had just about enough of this conversation anyway. I picked up, hoping it was Damon.

Wrong.

"Hello. This is Ronald Rheece calling; may I please speak to Elizabeth Wakefield?"

"Hold on, Ronald. She's right here." I handed the telephone to Elizabeth and said, "Here—it's your *boyfriend*," under my breath.

I almost felt like throwing the phone at her! I didn't know who I was more angry with:

Jessica

Ronald, for asking Elizabeth to the dance and ruining everything? Or Elizabeth, for saying *yes* and ruining everything!

Maybe they deserved each other.

Elizabeth

My heart sank as I wandered to my room with the cordless phone to my ear. I had been hoping more than anything that Blue would be the one calling me, not Ronald. Not that I thought Blue would want to talk to me since I'd blown him off twice that day at school. But I could hope. Right?

"Good evening, Elizabeth!" Ronald said.

"Hi, Ronald," I replied, trying really hard to be polite.

All the things Jessica had just said were flooding my brain. Her theory was totally ridiculous. Just because *she* couldn't understand not wanting to hurt Ronald's feelings didn't mean I was using this dance date with Ronald to avoid me and Blue. I wouldn't do that. I *couldn't* do that. I liked Blue too much!

"I'm calling because I was concerned about you, Elizabeth." Ronald cleared his throat. "I was wondering how your visit to the nurse turned out. I hope you're not coming down with something."

"Oh no—I'm fine. I didn't end up going, actually," Elizabeth said. "Thanks for asking, though."

"But your stomach—," Ronald went on.

"I get like that sometimes," I said. *Especially when a ham-and-egg-salad sandwich with onions is shoved under my nose!* "It's no big deal. Don't worry about it."

"Well, that's a relief," Ronald said. "If you got the flu now, that would be very poor timing. It would be very unpleasant if you were to throw up on me while we danced."

I laughed as I pictured the scene. Ronald might not be my first choice for a dance partner, but at least he could be amusing. Even though he wasn't really trying to be. "Don't worry, I promise I won't get sick. So, is that why you were calling? Because I should probably get back to my homework."

"Actually, I was hoping you'd be all finished with that," Ronald said. "I thought perhaps if your stomach was feeling better, you could meet me for a dish of ice cream, or perhaps you don't like ice cream. In that case, how about a gelato?"

Right then I heard call waiting beep in.

"Hold on just a sec," I told Ronald, relieved for the chance to avoid his question. I pressed the button and clicked on to the new call. "Hello?"

"Liz? Is that you?"

My heart started pounding. It was Blue!

"Hi!" I said, thrilled to hear from him. "Hold on just a sec, okay? I have to say good-bye on the other line."

As I told Ronald I had to go and that I'd see him at school tomorrow, my mind started working on the next conversation: I was going to have to tell Blue about my date with Ronald. I couldn't run away from it again.

Blue

Score!

I was so psyched when Elizabeth answered the phone and said she was going to get rid of the other call—not mine. Of course, that didn't mean she was going to tell me what I wanted to hear. But I hoped she was.

While I waited for her, I fiddled with a guitar pick that I'd left on the kitchen counter. This wasn't going to be the easiest conversation we'd ever had. But at least whenever you talk to Elizabeth on the phone, she always makes it really clear that she's totally focused on *you*. That's one of the things I really like about her. She doesn't sit and watch TV and just sort of go "uh-huh" after you tell her stuff. She *listens*.

There was a little click, and she came back on the line. "Hey, Blue! Sorry about that. How are you?" she asked.

"I'm okay, how about you?" I asked.

"I'm fine," she said.

Then there was this awkward pause that felt

like it lasted about ten minutes—but was probably more like five seconds. *Here goes nothing,* I told myself.

"So I was wondering," I said, trying to sound casual. "At school today, it kind of seemed like you were trying to, um, avoid me. If I did something wrong, could you maybe tell me so I can apologize?"

"No! It isn't anything you did," Elizabeth said quickly. "I'm sorry about that. I didn't mean to avoid you." She sighed. "It's just . . . I guess I had a lot on my mind."

I slumped against the kitchen counter in relief. At least Elizabeth wasn't mad at me.

"Well, you know you can tell me anything. You know, whenever you want to talk about it, I'm here," I assured her.

"Thanks, Blue," Elizabeth said. Was it me, or did that sound a little halfhearted? *Nah,* she was obviously just a little bummed out about something. Well, maybe what I had to say next would cheer her up. I *hoped* it would.

"Not to change the subject, but I was also calling for another reason. I was wondering if, um, you maybe wanted to go to the eighth-grade formal with me?" I paused. *There,* I'd said it.

Elizabeth was completely silent. I couldn't even hear her breathing. "Liz?" I said, my voice cracking a bit from nervousness. I was getting this sinking feeling—like the one I usually get before I wipe out on my surfboard. I finally heard her suck in a deep breath.

"I want to—more than anything," she replied. *Whew.* That was a good start. "But I can't."

Denied!

"Um, why not?" I managed to ask, when it seemed like she wasn't going to say more.

"I can't go to the dance with you because I agreed to go with someone else," Elizabeth finally blurted out.

Ouch! I threw the guitar pick across the kitchen. What was she doing, going with someone else? This was totally wrong.

"I know this will sound dumb," she said shyly. "But I really wanted to go to the dance with you. I was hoping that you'd ask me today, actually."

Okay, so maybe things weren't as bad as they seemed. We had been thinking the same exact thing. "I was going to," I said. "That's why I kept trying to find you—like at lunch."

Elizabeth sighed loudly, sounding frustrated. "But as soon as I got to school, Ronald Rheece asked me. I was so surprised that I couldn't think of how to tell him no, and I didn't want to hurt his feelings, so before I knew what I was doing—I . . . said yes."

"Ronald Rheece? Are you serious?" I asked. I tried not to laugh. Ronald isn't exactly the coolest guy at school. If Elizabeth *did* have to go with another guy, at least it wasn't one I was worried about competing with. I tried to picture Elizabeth and Ronald dancing together.

No. I couldn't picture it.

"I'm so sorry I messed things up," Elizabeth said. "I really wanted us to go together."

I felt this huge grin spreading across my face. I don't know why I was so happy. Things weren't exactly turning out the way I wanted them to. But just hearing Elizabeth say that she wanted to go to the dance with me and hearing how sad she was that she couldn't—that sort of made up for her accepting the date with Ronald.

Anyway, how could I be mad at her when she was only trying not to hurt the guy's feelings? The fact that she was so nice to everyone was another one of the things I liked about her.

"Blue? Are you still there?" she asked in a soft voice. "Do you hate me? Say something!"

"Sorry—I was just thinking," I said.

"About what?" she asked.

"That you're a good person," I said. "Even *if* you're going to the formal with the *wrong* person." I could feel myself blushing. Elizabeth and I had never been this open about liking each other before, and it felt a little scary. But it also felt good.

"So you're not mad?" Elizabeth asked.

"No—just disappointed," I said honestly. "I can't believe I lost out to Ronald Rheece by like a couple of hours. I should have just called you over the weekend, but Leaf and I were really busy doing all this work around the house, and, I dunno. I thought it would be easier to do it face-to-face." I could have kicked myself now. Instead I kicked the base of the kitchen counter. "Was that stupid or what?"

"I should have called and asked *you,*" Elizabeth said. "It's just as much my fault."

"Well, I guess we shouldn't procrastinate so much the next time we want to go to a dance together."

There was another semilong awkward pause. Then I said, "Hey, do you think Ronald would freak out if we danced together? Just one slow dance? I mean, just because you're going with him doesn't mean you have to stand next to him all night and dance to every single song with him," I added. "Right?"

Elizabeth laughed. "No, definitely not! We're going as friends."

"So it's settled," I said. "You'll show up with Ronald. He'll be your official date. But I'll be there too—by myself. And you and I *will* dance together—at least once. Okay?"

Elizabeth laughed again. "Sounds like a plan!"

I smiled. I wasn't looking forward to standing around waiting for my opportunity to hang out with Elizabeth when what I wanted to do was spend the whole evening with her. But I'd take what I could get. If that was only one measly dance, then so be it. I guess.

Jameel

Maybe I'm too impatient. That's one of the things my dad's always saying I need to work on. And maybe Dad's right.

It was up to Bethel to ask me to the eighth-grade formal. And I knew that. But here I was, looking for her in the cafeteria, dying to talk to her.

I really wanted to go to the dance with Bethel. And if she wasn't going to ask me, then I was going to help her ask me. In a very, very roundabout way. She *couldn't* avoid the topic any longer. She *wouldn't*. I was going to make it so she *had* to bring it up.

I spotted her sitting near the west exit and smiled. Then I hurried over with my tray. This was actually sort of fun.

"Hey, Bethel!" I said excitedly.

"Oh, hi, Jameel," she said. Right away she started looking a little nervous. *Does she know what I'm up to?* I wondered. She slid her lunch over to make room for mine, but I could tell she wasn't all that thrilled to see me. Or maybe she *was,* and that's what was making her act embarrassed. I tried to tell myself the second one was true.

"All right, so you're not going to believe this," I said as I opened my carton of milk.

Bethel raised one eyebrow as she looked up from her fruit salad. "What am I not going to believe?"

"I got tickets to an LA Sparks game! They're playing the Phoenix Mercury." Bethel loved watching the WNBA on TV, so I knew she'd want to see them in person. "Isn't that great?"

Her eyes lit up. "Tickets to see the Sparks? That's awesome. How did you get them?"

Actually, I didn't, I thought. I hoped she wasn't going to say yes and call my bluff. Hoped? No, that wasn't a strong enough word. I counted on it! "It was easy. I just called the ticket office," I said. *Don't ask me what the number is,* I thought. Because my research didn't go that far. All I did was see the Sparks' schedule in the newspaper and decide to take a chance.

I picked up a french fry. "Actually, my dad paid for it—it was his credit card. I was just the one with the brilliant idea."

"So you're going with your parents?" Bethel looked like she was trying to be happy for me, but her face registered sheer disappointment.

Jameel

Did she really think I'd mention a Sparks game and *not* invite her?

"Well, yeah, but that's because we need someone to drive," I said. "Unless you got your license without telling me?"

"We? You mean . . . you got a ticket for me?" Bethel asked.

"Of course," I said. "We got four tickets. I told my mom and dad that if you *couldn't* go, for some bizarre reason, it would be easy to find someone else. But I hope you can because for one thing, you know the team's roster better than me. And for another, you owe me a popcorn from the last track meet we went to—"

Bethel started laughing. "Hold on—I don't owe you anything!"

"Sure, you do," I said. "Don't you remember?"

Bethel shook her head. "No."

"Then you can't say it didn't happen. Can you?" I teased.

"Okay, but hold on. You haven't mentioned when the game is, so how do I know if I can even go?" Bethel asked.

"Oh, did I forget to mention that?" I asked casually. *Here we go,* I thought. *Here's where I give her the perfect chance to invite me to the formal.* Because as much as Bethel loved the WNBA, I had a feeling she wouldn't miss the biggest dance of the year for anything. Don't get me wrong—she's not a girlie girl, but Bethel *loves* to dance. "It's this Saturday night," I said as I looked straight into her eyes.

Bethel flinched—not much, but just enough to notice. She moved back in her seat and turned a little to one side so she wasn't looking right at me. Then she bit her lip and started fiddling with her napkin.

It was just the reaction I was hoping for. Bethel knew *I* knew how much she loved the Sparks. And she knew she'd have to give me a good reason for missing the game. So she'd just *have* to bring up the dance. And that would mean she'd either have to tell me she was planning to go without me or that she'd been hoping to go *with* me.

If she didn't say it right off the bat, well, I'd drag it out of her.

"Bethel?" I asked. "Did you hear me?"

"Yeah. Of course," she said in a quiet voice. "Um, Saturday night. The game."

"Well? You can go, right? Unless you have other plans . . ." *Say you can't go!* I thought. *Say you'll have to turn me down because you do have plans for Saturday night and, while you're on the subject, you were actually hoping I'd want to go to the formal with you! Come on! I just gave you another perfect opening!*

Jameel

Can you hope for something so much that you jinx your chances?

Bethel suddenly stood up. "I'll have to ask my parents and, um, get back to you. Okay?" She grabbed her tray and darted away. If I hadn't already known that Bethel was an amazing sprinter, I would have guessed it then. She was moving away from me at lightning speed!

So much for the perfect opening. So much for making it easy for her to ask me. She was totally doing everything possible *not* to ask me! And I *knew* the girl liked me.

I was starting to get suspicious. Had she already invited someone else to the formal? Or was she allergic to school dances? I knew it was pretty unusual for girls in our school to date boys who were younger than them, not to mention shorter. Was *that* what was bothering her?

Was Bethel ashamed of me?

Elizabeth

"So what do you guys think about covering the formal?" Brian asked on Tuesday afternoon. "Is it too light of a story for us to do?"

"I don't think so," I said. "As long as it doesn't take up the whole issue."

"Ooh, that will be so exciting," Salvador crooned, folding his hands together daintily. "The biggest scandal of the evening, ladies and gentlemen, was when Miss Anna Wang was seen wearing pink shoes with a *black* dress. It was too daring for words!"

"Come on, we'd never do that!" I interrupted him, laughing.

It was kind of a relief to be sitting in the *Zone* office and eating my lunch, to tell you the truth. There were two reasons I was psyched to be there.

Ronald had asked me if I wanted to spend study hall together again. I was happy to use the meeting as an excuse.

I love working on *Zone*. It's a 'zine that Anna,

Salvador, and I started at the beginning of the year—all by ourselves. And I'm really proud of it.

Usually there's another reason I like to be there. Blue joined the staff a couple of months ago, and it's always great to see him and bounce ideas back and forth. But he wasn't here today, for some reason. He was probably skipping out so he could study—which he does from time to time since he's been working on keeping his grades up.

"Well, Liz, what sort of dress are you going to wear?" Salvador asked. "Come on, we need to get this special dance-fashion issue started. Will it be a designer or—"

"Who cares what she's wearing? I'm more interested in who she's going with," Anna said, bursting through the door right at that moment. "Sorry I'm late. Anyway," she said breathlessly, turning to me. "I heard a rumor this morning, and I can't believe it's true."

Salvador sat up straighter and looked across the table at me. "What's the big rumor?" he asked.

"I don't know," I said. "If it's about me, nobody would tell me, right?" I joked. This was starting to feel sort of awkward all of a sudden. I was really embarrassed!

"I heard you're going to the dance with

Ronald Rheece," Anna said, her eyes widening for emphasis. "Is that true?"

"Ronald? Oh, I thought she was going to say you were going with Blue," Salvador said, looking confused and, for some reason, a little relieved.

"I was going to. I mean, that's sort of what I planned," I admitted. It felt weird to be talking about all this with Salvador and Brian sitting there. I can't really explain why. "But he didn't ask me until after Ronald had asked me, and I'd already said yes, so—"

"Wait a second. You really did say yes to Ronald?" Brian asked.

"It's not like it sounds," I said. "He just asked me to go, and I felt like it would be rude to say no without a good excuse. And, well, I didn't have a good excuse."

Salvador put down his sandwich. "Okay, let me get this straight. You and Ronald. Dancing together at the eighth-grade formal. Not just dancing—spending the whole romantic evening together?"

"Well, yeah, I guess we'll be spending the evening together. That's not so bad, is it?" I asked, looking around at everyone.

"No." Brian shrugged. "If you don't mind spending your entire eighth-grade formal discussing geometry theorems." Whoa, that was pretty harsh coming from Brian, who's one of the nicest guys I know.

"Come on, that would never happen," Anna said.

"It wouldn't?" Brian asked.

"No, because Ronald is way past geometry," Salvador said.

They all started to laugh. For the next several minutes they kept making jokes about what a boring night I was going to have at the formal. I sat there and ate my lunch and ignored them. Or tried to. After a while it was really getting on my nerves. I decided to try to change the topic.

"So can we get back to what sort of coverage we're going to give the formal?" I asked. "Because Jessica's thinking of bringing our dad's digital camera to the dance on Saturday. If he lets us, which is sort of doubtful, we could take pictures and then download them onto the Web site."

"Oh yeah. We definitely want to capture any intimate moments between you and Ronald and put them on the Web," Salvador teased.

"Okay, so enough about *me*," I said, feeling really annoyed with Salvador. "Who are *you* taking to the formal?" I looked right into his eyes and challenged him. "Your grandmother?"

Salvador lives with his grandmother because his parents are in the military and travel around a lot.

Salvador just looked right back at me. He seemed sort of put out at first, and I was starting to feel bad for teasing him. But if he was going to dish it out, then he had to take it too.

Then he broke into a typical Sal-like grin. "Well, now that you mention it, sure. That's actually a great idea. I'll ask the Doña to the dance."

"Come on, be serious," Brian said.

"I'm completely serious," Salvador said. He sat back in his chair and put his hands behind his head. "I bet she'd love to come."

"Yeah, but . . . she's your grandmother," Anna said. "Isn't that going to be sort of bizarre? Do you think she'd have any fun?"

"Of course! She'll be with me. And check this out—the teachers will all love me because it's like having an extra chaperon, for free," Salvador said. "I'll earn *major* brownie points with this. Besides, the Doña could use a little fun in her life." Right. The Doña probably had more fun in her life than all of us put together.

"And you're a fun date?" Anna asked. "Says who?"

"I can't think of a better dancer than the Doña," I said. "Remember when we saw her dance with Mr. Fox? She was *amazing.*" Mr. Fox was the best dance teacher in Sweet Valley. Anna nodded enthusiastically.

I suddenly remembered dancing with Salvador

a few months ago at a dance-a-thon to benefit the hospital. It was held at the Sweet Valley Community Center. We'd shared one slow dance, and things had gotten sort of weird between us because we ended up staring into each other's eyes in this really romantic-seeming setting. It was one of the times I'd thought maybe there was something between me and Salvador. Even though we've kissed a couple of times, we were definitely beyond that now.

That same night Salvador had interrupted our semiromantic moment by going nuts, dancing the tango with me, then cutting in on Brian and Anna—and actually dancing with Brian! I wondered if he was planning another wild night like that.

"Bringing the Doña sounds pretty cool, actually," Brian said.

"So there." Salvador looked right at me. "You can go ahead and make fun of my date if you want, but I wouldn't recommend it. The Doña tends to take things personally."

"I wasn't trying to make fun of you," I said. "I was just trying to get you to quit teasing me about going to the dance with Ronald."

There was this really uncomfortable thirty seconds or so while we all sat there at the table, not saying anything. I could almost bet that

Salvador was thinking of ten more jokes to make about me going with Ronald, but at least he was keeping them to himself this time.

"Liz, I'm dying for a soda," Anna said suddenly. "Want to come with me? You guys want anything?" She pushed back her chair and stood up.

"Could you get me a root beer?" Brian handed Anna some change.

"When we get back, we're deciding what goes in the next issue," Anna declared. "Could you guys start brainstorming a list of things while we're gone?"

"Yes, master," Salvador said as he half bowed to her.

I followed Anna outside into the hallway.

"Okay, so I'm really not thirsty," Anna admitted as we started walking down the hall. "But I had to ask you in private, away from those guys. How does Blue feel about all this? I mean, I know you really wanted to go with him. . . ."

I nodded. "Definitely. It was so stupid of me because I was waiting for him to ask me. Why didn't I just ask him?"

"I don't know. Fear of rejection?" Anna said. "I know that before I asked Toby, I was *sooo* nervous."

"*You* asked *Toby*? That's so awesome," I said.

"Well, you know I'm a modern woman," Anna replied, tossing her head and grinning. "But it would have been even *more* awesome if you and Blue were going together. I really wanted all of us to be there together. Not that we won't still have fun, but I just really thought it would be a big night for you and Blue. You know, to really be on a date for the first time."

I sighed. "I wish I'd never said yes to Ronald, but there's nothing I can do about it now."

"I don't know." Anna and I stopped in front of the vending machine. "Maybe there is."

I started feeding a dollar bill into the slot. "Like what?"

"Well, just because you and Blue aren't going together *technically* doesn't mean you can't still be each other's date. You know, you could be each other's *secret* date."

My soda can rattled out into the bottom, and I grabbed it while she put quarters into the machine for Brian's root beer. I wasn't sure if I liked Anna's idea. I wasn't sure if I even understood it!

"Doesn't that sound romantic? You'd be, like, pledged to each other, but nobody would know about it. Which reminds me—who is Blue taking to the formal?" Anna asked.

"He said he's just going to go by himself and try to get a dance with me," I said with a shrug.

"Wow. That's so sweet!" Anna said. "You *have* to do the secret-date thing."

I wanted to agree with Anna. But wouldn't that be really unfair to Ronald? I was supposed to be *his* date, not Blue's. But then, I couldn't help it if I'd be thinking of Blue the whole night. And if I was going to be thinking of him the whole night, he might as well be my secret date.

Maybe the dance wasn't going to be such a disaster after all!

Blue

Wednesday afternoon, I peeked through the window on the gym door. If Elizabeth was inside, I'd go in and help. If not . . . well, I could think of things I'd rather do with my afternoon than make decorations. Not that I have anything against decorations. They're just not all that thrilling when you compare them to, say, playing the guitar, or video games, or surfing.

I saw Toby and Anna first. Then I spotted Elizabeth over on the other side of the gym, by herself. Yes! Maybe this wouldn't be my favorite way to spend the afternoon, but at least I'd be hanging out with Elizabeth. I'd hardly seen her all week.

I pushed open the door and walked past Kristin, who was sitting at a small folding table, assigning people to different jobs as they came in.

"Hey," I said when I saw Brian standing next to her. Brian's in our band too, and we hang out a lot. "How's it going?"

"Hey, Blue," he replied. "What's up?"

"Hi," Kristin said with a big smile. "Here to help?"

"Definitely," I said.

"That's great! Well, let's see, we need people to make dried-flower centerpieces for the tables." Kristin tapped her pen against a clipboard. "And we're short a couple of people at the glitter-and-papier-mâché station."

I cleared my throat. Neither one of those sounded exactly like my type of creative project. "Uh, is it okay if I go help with whatever Liz is working on?"

Kristin smiled wryly. "Sure. If you can handle making lantern chains from aluminum foil?"

"Dude, those are my specialty!" I joked. "How did you know?"

Brian and Kristin chuckled as I walked away.

"So. How many rolls of aluminum foil does it take to make one lantern?" I asked as I walked up to Elizabeth.

She looked up when she heard my voice, and her pretty blue-green eyes lit up as a giant smile spread across her face. Her smile always makes my heart feel like it's beating at three times the regular speed. "I don't know," she said. "But it takes more than one person. Look at this!" She held up a crumpled ball of foil.

"Liz, we're supposed to make lanterns, not lightbulbs," I teased her.

She laughed and picked up a sheet of paper from the folding table in front of her. "Here's the diagram. Can *you* figure it out?"

I held up the piece of paper and tried to read it. Then I turned it to one side, then I turned it upside down. "Okay, I think I've got it."

Elizabeth laughed again. "Okay. So what do we do first?"

I laid out a few sheets of aluminum foil and started to fold them according to the directions. We worked together in silence for about five minutes until we had our first chain made. Once we got the hang of it, they started to go really quickly. Then we started making small talk.

"Kristin told me they're going to have lights shining on these," Elizabeth said as we made our second chain. "So they should look really neat for the dance."

"She's really going all out for this," I said.

"Yeah. She's a good class president, don't you think?" Elizabeth asked.

"Definitely," I said. "It takes someone with a lot of energy and, um, school spirit. Whatever that means. I always thought that was a totally weird term, you know? Like it's a ghost. The School Spirit. It shows up to haunt people at school dances and football games."

Elizabeth laughed. Then we were quiet again

for a couple of minutes until she said, "Blue? I had this idea yesterday, and I wanted to know what you think."

"Okay, shoot," I said.

"Well, it's about the dance," she said quietly. "I know I'm going with Ronald. Officially and all. But what would you think of us being . . . I don't know." Her face turned sort of pink. "Secret dates?"

I wasn't totally sure what she meant. "Secret dates?" I asked.

"Well, we won't really be there together," she said. "But secretly we can think of each other as our date. Like, I'll still think of you as my date. Even though I'm going with Ronald. Does that make sense?"

I grinned. "It makes perfect sense. So even though it might look like I'm there alone, I won't be?"

"Right." Elizabeth smiled at me. "It's not perfect, but it's better than nothing."

"Definitely!" I said.

Behind us, I heard someone dragging something across the gym floor. I turned around and saw Ronald trying to position a ladder next to our table.

"Excuse me, Blue? Elizabeth? Could I have a little assistance?" he asked.

Great, I thought. *Why does he have to show up*

now? His timing is awful. "Sure thing!" I said. "What do you need?"

"Well, Kristin asked me to help hang the lantern chains you're making," Ronald said. "So if you can assist me in getting this ladder set in the right place, that would be very helpful." He looked at Elizabeth, who was holding one of our lantern chains. "Beautiful work, Elizabeth," he said. "I didn't know you were creative and artistic, on top of your other good features."

I tried not to groan as I unfolded the ladder and pressed the metal hinge down to lock it in place.

"Um, thanks," Elizabeth said. I could tell she felt as frustrated about Ronald showing up to "help" as I did.

"You know, Blue," Ronald said as he came over to me. "I didn't want to admit this to Kristin. But I'm actually just a wee bit afraid of heights. Would you mind climbing the ladder instead of me?"

And leave you down here to hang out with Liz instead of me? I thought. *No way!* But I couldn't say that.

All I could think was, *Is this how the night of the formal is going to be? Whenever Liz and I end up talking, is Ronald going to materialize right in the middle of us?*

Why had he asked Elizabeth to the dance anyway? Did he really have a crush on her? She was interested in *me*. Couldn't he see that? It seemed to be so obvious to everyone else.

I looked around the gym, desperate to find another place for Ronald to hang out.

"You know, Ronald, if you're really afraid of heights, maybe you should go help out at another workstation," I said. "Liz and I can handle this—we'll make some more chains, then I'll hang them up."

"What are you saying?" Ronald asked.

"We really appreciate your help, man," I said. "But don't you think that someone with your obvious skills should put their *mind* to work here?"

Ronald looked at me with a confused expression. "What are you trying to imply?"

"Well, you're really good at math, right? Including geometry? And Kristin is sitting over there trying to draw circles or squares or—I can't even tell what they are. Which shows you that she could really use your help."

Ronald frowned. "You know, I can see what you're trying to do," he said.

"Oh?" I asked, trying to sound innocent. "What's that?"

"You're trying to get rid of me," Ronald said.

I saw this really concerned look pass across Elizabeth's face. Then she opened her mouth to say something.

I jumped in ahead of her. "I'm not trying to

get rid of you," I said. "Why would you say that?" *Because it's true? Because I'd really rather be alone with Liz right now?*

"Oh, it's nothing personal." Ronald scooted over so he was standing even closer to Elizabeth. "It's just that I know better than to leave Elizabeth alone with another guy. I was lucky enough to convince her to attend the formal with me." He laughed awkwardly. "Do you think I'd actually let her out of my sight around a cool surfer dude like you?"

I let out a fake chuckle to let Ronald know I thought he was joking, but inside I was feeling pretty riled up. And that's totally out of the ordinary for someone like me. I knew I was being rude, but I just couldn't believe that I was having to fight with Ronald Rheece for the girl of my dreams! Not that he's not a decent guy, but he's not exactly Elizabeth's type!

Poor Elizabeth, I thought. She would have to spend hours and hours with Ronald on Saturday night. I looked at her and smiled. If I could change things, I would. But it was out of my hands!

Bethel

"So, Bethel. Are you bringing anyone to the formal? Or are you coming by yourself?" Jessica asked as she sprinkled silver glitter onto the giant sign we were making in the gym on Wednesday afternoon.

It was a totally innocent question. She didn't mean anything by it, and she was only being nice. But I felt myself start to get completely nervous.

"So far?" I asked. "I'm coming by myself." I squeezed more glue onto the poster board.

"That's cool," Jessica said. "A lot of people are doing that."

"You're going with Damon, right?" I asked.

"Yeah." A huge smile spread across Jessica's face. She and Damon were so happy together. I felt this little pang. Would Jameel and I ever be as happy as Damon and Jessica?

But that's ridiculous, I told myself. Damon and Jessica had been going out for a long time. I couldn't even manage to ask Jameel to one lousy formal.

"So whose heart did you break?" Jessica asked.

"What do you mean?"

"Well, who asked you to the dance? I'm sure you've had to turn down a few offers," Jessica said.

Talk about a good friend! Jessica had total confidence in me even when *I* didn't.

I shrugged. "Nope. Nobody asked me."

"Really?" Jessica looked surprised. "Wait a second. I know why! It's because the person who *really* wants to ask you isn't *in* the eighth grade. Is he?"

"Who are you all of a sudden? Sherlock Holmes?" I teased, threatening to squirt glue on her shirt.

"Hey, can I help it if I'm clairvoyant?" Jessica asked. "So, spill. Why didn't you invite Jameel? Did you guys have a fight or something?"

"Hmmm. Not exactly," I said. "I sort of, well, I sort of haven't invited him yet."

"What are you waiting for? The dance is only three days away."

"I know!" I said. "I just haven't had a chance."

Jessica raised one eyebrow and sort of frowned at me. "I saw you guys having lunch yesterday."

Busted.

"So ask him," Jessica said. "What are you so worried about? He'll say yes. Besides, what do you have to lose?"

I shrugged. Then I squirted some of the glue I was holding onto the tip of my thumb.

Jessica watched what I was doing for a moment, then stood up abruptly and dusted off her hands. "Come on."

"What?" I looked up, confused.

"You're going to call him right now." She took my hands and started yanking at my arms. Groaning, I let her pull me up. Jessica can be really pushy when she wants to be.

"But he already has plans for that night," I pleaded.

Jessica kept pulling me toward the door. "So he'll have to break them," she said matter-of-factly.

I hope she's right, I thought as I went out into the hallway. There was a pay phone right outside the gym—a few of them, actually. I took some change from my pocket and dialed Jameel's house. *Please be home. Please be home,* I thought as I listened to the first two rings. If he didn't answer soon, I was going to lose my nerve.

"Hello?" Jameel said.

"Hey!" I said excitedly. "It's Bethel." I glanced quickly over at Jessica, who was grinning from ear to ear.

"Oh, hi," he said. He sounded a little bored.

"So how are you?" I asked.

"Fine."

"Um, what are you up to?" I pressed, starting to feel a little awkward.

"Nothing."

Whoa. It wasn't like Jameel to give one-word answers. Usually he launched into some funny story; half the time it was hard for me to even get a word in edgewise. But I wasn't going to let that stop me. Maybe he was only tired, and I'd caught him in the middle of a nap or something.

"You're probably wondering why I'm calling," I said. "I'm still at school. We're making decorations for the dance this Saturday," I explained.

"Uh-huh," Jameel said. He couldn't have sounded less interested if he tried.

"And I realized something," I went on, ignoring his bad mood. "Actually, I've been thinking about it for a while. You know, Jameel, I'd really like it if you would go to the eighth-grade formal with me this Saturday."

I bit my lip, waiting for his answer. I don't know what I was expecting: for him to shout, "Yes!" or for him to say, "I thought you'd never ask," or some sort of romantic thing. But I *wasn't* expecting total silence on the other end of the phone.

"Jameel?" I finally said. "Did you hear me?"

"Mmm-hmm," he replied.

"Did I call at a bad time? I'm sorry," I said,

feeling so awkward, I wished I'd never picked up the phone.

"No, it's not a bad time. It's just . . ." Jameel paused.

"What?" I asked.

"Well, I feel like you're only asking me this now because you know I have tickets to that basketball game on Saturday night," Jameel said. "So now you can ask me and you know I can't go."

"But . . . is it really too late?" I asked. "Couldn't you exchange the tickets for another game or—"

"That's not the point," Jameel said. "If you really wanted me to go to the dance with you, you would have asked me already. You could have asked me at lunch yesterday when I mentioned getting the Sparks tickets!"

"Yeah, I know," I said. "But . . ." What could I say? That I was a complete chicken?

"So why didn't you?" Jameel pressed.

"I—I don't know," I stammered, feeling suddenly defensive—even though I knew this was kind of my fault. But still, didn't Jameel realize it took a lot of guts for me to ask him to the dance? And now he was acting like I was the biggest jerk in the universe because I hadn't asked him earlier! "Look," I said, "if you don't want to go, fine. See you later." I hung up the telephone without waiting for a reply and leaned against the wall. I didn't have to worry about being too tall for Jameel or being a year older than him. Because Jameel wasn't going with me, *period*.

And even though I was mad at him right now, I knew I had only myself to blame!

Jameel

I hit the off button and dropped the cordless onto the coffee table.

Why didn't I just say yes when Bethel called to invite me? That was what I wanted, right? So why did I insist on proving some sort of dumb point about *when* she should have asked me? The point was that she finally had! So why hadn't I said yes?

I don't know. I guess I'm not very good at this yet. I thought that if I told her I was hurt she hadn't invited me before, she would beg me to go with her. I wanted her to apologize for waiting so long to ask me. Instead she'd hung up!

Smooth, Jameel, I told myself. *Real smooth.* Now what was I going to do? I had no WNBA tickets and no date with Bethel.

Blue

I was so psyched to get home in time to go surfing. Not that hanging foil-covered chains in the gym hadn't been fun. Hey, anything with Elizabeth is usually fun. But with Ronald hovering at our side the whole time? Anyway, a full day of classes is more than enough time to be at school. And I hadn't been able to get down to the ocean all week.

My big brother, Leaf, was there hanging out with some of his high-school buddies, competing to see who could catch the biggest wave and ride it the longest, as usual. But I wasn't in a competing mood. I wanted to enjoy some time by myself. Just me, my board, the water.

I was paddling out to catch my next wave when I spotted a friend paddling out about twenty feet away. "Tanya!" I said, heading over toward her, suddenly forgetting my plan to spend some time by myself. My board floated up over a huge wave as I paddled in her direction.

"Hey!" Tanya Papadakalis replied, heading my

way. We met up halfway in between our original spots.

"How's it going?" I asked her. "Been out here long?"

"No, I just got here," Tanya said. "I had to stay after school for detention." She groaned. "Can you believe it? Me?"

I laughed. "Actually, yeah." Tanya had a reputation for being sort of a class clown.

"So what's up? Anything new?" Tanya asked.

"Not much, really," I told her.

"Hey, did you know that movie *Cowabunga!* is opening on Friday night?" Tanya asked. "It looks totally stupid, but I'll probably go anyway, just for the surf scenes."

I laughed, thinking of how bogus the movie's title was. "Yeah, me too."

I'd always really liked hanging out and talking with Tanya. And suddenly this thought occurred to me. Tanya and I had fun together, and we were totally friends. Maybe she could help with my Ronald Rheece situation.

"Hey, Tanya," I said, giving her a sly grin. "What are you doing on Saturday night?"

Elizabeth

I was right in the middle of my favorite sitcom on Wednesday night when the phone rang. *If this is Ronald again, I'm telling him I can't get any calls after seven-thirty—my parents' rules,* I decided as I reached for the phone. He'd called twice already to discuss "coordinating dressing options" for the dance. What now? Did he want to talk about what we should *say* to each other on Saturday night? He really believed in planning everything down to the last detail. He was the complete opposite of Blue!

"Hello?" I said.

"Hey, Liz, it's Blue."

I heaved a sigh of relief. "I'm so glad it's you!"

"Oh yeah? Well, cool," Blue said. "Who did you think it was going to be?"

"I probably shouldn't say this. But I thought it might be Ronald." I felt bad for complaining about Ronald, but I couldn't help it. He was driving me crazy!

"Yeah, that's kind of why I'm calling," Blue

said. "You know the way Ronald was sort of attached to you at the gym today?"

"Yeah, sorry about that," I said, thinking of how agitated Blue had been at the gym earlier. "I honestly don't know why he's acting like that all of a sudden."

"He's taking this dance thing pretty seriously," Blue said. "I like your secret-date plan and all, but I doubt I'm going to get within twenty feet of you on Saturday night."

"What?" I laughed. "Come on, it won't be that bad."

"Liz? Do you remember when you went to get a drink of water? He wouldn't even let you do *that* by yourself," Blue reminded me.

"Yeah. Do you know how hard it is to get a drink from the water fountain when there's somebody hovering over you, telling you how to tilt your head for maximum water access?" I asked with a laugh. "You know, maybe I should say something to him," I suggested, turning serious.

"Nah, don't hurt his feelings—I mean, he's trying to be nice, I guess," Blue said. "Anyway, I think I have a solution to make Ronald less suspicious of you and me. And that way we might be able to get at least one dance together. Maybe."

"Really?" I asked, feeling excited. The fact that Blue had actually been spending time on this made me feel really good. "So what's your plan?"

"I'm going to bring a date to the dance too," Blue said.

"Oh?" I asked, suddenly tensing up. What was he getting at?

"Is that okay with you?" Blue asked. "I sort of already invited her, though, so . . . man, maybe I should have run this past you first?"

"No, that's okay," I assured him, even though I wasn't quite sure if it was okay or not. "Who did you invite?"

"You don't know her," Blue began. "Her name is Tanya Papadakalis. She's a surfer friend of mine, from the beach."

So far this didn't sound too bad. I mean, did I really have to worry about someone named "Tanya Papadakalis"? Not likely. Then again, a lot of the girl surfers I'd seen when Blue was teaching me how to surf had been really, really pretty. "So where does she go to school?" I asked.

"Sweet Valley Middle School," Blue said. "She's new to the school this year, though, so you probably didn't know her when you were there. Anyway, she's totally cool. You guys will get along great."

"So we can make this sort of a . . . double date?" I asked. "Only we'll try to switch partners?" Was this getting too complicated to work?

It sounded like one of those really disastrous square dances we'd had back in the sixth grade. I could hear our old gym teacher now: "Change your partner, do-si-do. . . ."

"Exactly! See, Ronald will think I'm with Tanya. Which I will be, technically," Blue explained. "But I'll really be your date, just like you'll really be mine. And having her along will distract Ronald from watching our every move. And get this! Tanya already volunteered to dance with Ronald so you and I can be alone."

Hey, maybe he really is on to something, I thought. Tanya was starting to sound like an angel who had come to our rescue! "You know what, Blue? This just might work," I said.

"I was hoping you'd say that." He laughed. "Hey, Liz, next time we go to a school dance? Let's try not to do this again. Deal?"

I laughed too. I was so glad Blue and I were on the same wavelength! "Deal."

Jessica

"What's a deal?" I walked into the living room just as Elizabeth was hanging up the phone. "Oh no. You weren't talking to Ronald again, were you?"

"No, that was Blue." Elizabeth had a goofy, dreamy smile plastered to her face. It made me so happy to see her that way—she definitely deserved it! But if she was that happy, it could only mean one thing.

"Oh my God—Elizabeth, I didn't know you had it in you. You broke your date with Ronald, didn't you? You're going to the dance with Blue!"

"What?" Elizabeth looked at me like I was crazy. "No. What are you talking about? That would be so rude."

I rolled my eyes. "Like accepting a date with someone you don't like isn't rude?"

Elizabeth decided to ignore my little outburst.

"Okay, so why are you so happy, then?" I asked.

"Because Blue came up with a way we can

hang out together at the dance," she said. "He's going to bring another date, this girl Tanya Papadakalis, so that Ronald won't keep such a close eye on him and me and—"

"Wait, Liz," I interrupted. "I'm sorry, but did you just say Tanya Papadakalis? I *know* her." Why did Elizabeth sound so excited about this plan? If I were her, I'd be freaking out. Big time.

"You do?" Elizabeth asked. "What's she like? How do you know her?"

"I met her through a friend of Damon's. We all went out for pizza once," I said. Tanya's face popped into my head. "She has shiny brown, curly hair and olive skin, brown eyes. . . . Liz, she's totally pretty."

"Oh." Elizabeth shrugged. "Well, that's okay, I guess."

Why wasn't she getting upset? I would have been having a major anxiety attack if the guy I liked was going on a *date* with Tanya Papadakalis.

"On top of that, Tanya's also very smart and funny," I said. "In addition to being like the best surfer her age at the beach."

"Mmmm." Elizabeth nodded, her forehead wrinkling with worry. "Blue said she was a good surfer."

I waited a few seconds to let it all sink in.

Jessica

Elizabeth had been in such an upbeat mood when I walked in, obviously it was going to take a while for her to come back to earth. Not that I enjoyed being the one who had to tell her all this! It was just that she really needed to know what a bad idea this was.

She started to chew her lower lip while she fiddled with the fringe on one of the sofa pillows.

"So," I said. "Do you *still* think Blue bringing Tanya is a great plan?"

She frowned. "Maybe not. I don't know."

"Look, Liz, it's not that I think Blue likes anyone else but you. But you're practically forcing him into the arms of another woman." Not that I knew about that firsthand, but it sounded right.

"Jess, you watch way too many movies," Elizabeth snapped. Then she took a deep breath. "Look, Blue likes *me*. And I trust him. He's only doing all of this so we can spend time together anyway. So I don't care if Tanya looks like Cindy Crawford and is as smart as Albert Einstein. I'm not worried." Elizabeth bobbed her head on the final syllable for emphasis.

I looked at her skeptically. Something told me that Elizabeth was saying this stuff to convince herself, not me. But there was no use trying to pound the truth into her. I let out a huge sigh. "I hope you're right, Liz." I really did.

She's definitely right about one thing, though, I thought as I headed into the living room toward the VCR.

I probably do watch too many movies.

Elizabeth
Things Left to Do Before the Dance

Find shoes to match the dress I'm borrowing from Anna.

Borrow necklace from Jessica.

Get earrings back that Jessica borrowed two months ago.

Eliminate any and all insecure feelings about Tanya Papadakalis.

Figure out how to tell Ronald we're not dancing to any slow songs.

Jameel

"Bethel! Wait up!" I jogged after her as she walked up the school steps on Friday morning.

Bethel and Jessica were completely engaged in conversation, and I didn't exactly think Bethel was going to stop and wait for me. After all, she'd been avoiding me ever since Wednesday. She hadn't even waited around to talk to me after track practice on Thursday. That was pretty serious. If I wanted to make things up with her before the dance—or ever—I had a feeling I had to talk to her today.

"Hey, Bethel!" I called out, louder this time.

She turned around halfway up the steps and waited for me.

Don't blow it, I told myself as I smiled and walked up to her and Jessica. Bethel looked so cute in her short plaid skirt, sweater, and chunky loafers. Her hair was pulled back into a wide barrette, and she was wearing pretty gold hoop earrings. *Don't act like a jerk!*

Jameel

As I got closer, I could see that Jessica was giving me this critical look. In fact, she was practically glaring. *What did Bethel tell her?* I wondered. *Is the situation totally hopeless?*

"Hi, guys," I said. "What's up?" I looked at Jessica and then at Bethel.

"First-period algebra," Jessica muttered.

"Hey, at least it's Friday. Right?" I asked as I turned to Bethel. "The best day of the week when it comes to school." I smiled at her.

"Definitely." Bethel shifted her black leather backpack from one shoulder to the other. "So, are you getting psyched for your Sparks game on Saturday?"

I don't know why, but that was the *last* thing I expected her to say. I didn't know how to respond. Should I tell her that I never had any tickets? That I was only saying I did to get her to invite me to the dance?

"Oh yeah," I said. "Sure."

"We'd better go," Jessica said. "Didn't you have to pick up your algebra homework?"

"Oh. Yeah. Well, have a great time at the game," Bethel said, not even looking me in the eye. She gave me a little wave as she turned to go up the steps into the building.

"Bethel, wait," I said.

"Sorry—I've got to get to my locker before

class!" she called back over her shoulder.

She totally hates me, I thought as I stood on the steps in a daze. *Bethel regrets ever asking me to the dance. She'll never ask me to anything again. And I really like her. Now what am I supposed to do?*

Elizabeth

"Liz, is this straight?" Jessica asked as I passed by her and Damon. They were trying to hang a gigantic sparkle-covered paper sign on the wall.

"Hold your end up higher!" I told her.

"I told you it was crooked again," Damon said with a laugh. "Your sister does not know the meaning of a straight line."

Jessica giggled. "Can I help it if I'm geometrically challenged?"

"Good luck, you guys," I said as I kept walking. I needed more felt-tip markers, and Kristin had told me to check with Bethel. It was Friday after school, and we were all putting the final touches to the gym. Me, I was trying to keep Blue and Ronald from getting into yet another argument.

I finally found Bethel over by the east side of the gym. She was sitting behind a table, coloring name tags for the adult chaperons. She didn't look all that thrilled to be there.

"Hi, Bethel," I said. "Kristin said you might have some markers I could borrow."

"You can take them all," she said. "I'm almost done."

"Hey, those look really nice!" I pointed to the name tags she'd already made. She'd drawn swirls and flowers around each person's name. "That's kind of what I'm trying to do for the snack tables. I'm making paper tablecloths," I explained. I waited for her to finish the last tag. "So are you looking forward to tomorrow night?" I asked her.

"Yes . . . and no," she said, looking up at me. "See, I'm going by myself. And I really don't know if that's going to be fun or not. You know?"

"I think it'll be fun," I said. "I mean, that way you can hang out with friends and dance with whoever you want." I looked back across the gym at Ronald and Blue, who were waiting for me. I was amazed that Ronald had let me walk all the way across the gym by myself! He'd been tagging along everywhere all week.

"In fact, I think going by yourself is really cool," I told Bethel. *Much better than getting into a dumb, awkward situation like the one I'm in now!*

"It does sound cool," Bethel agreed. "I just wish . . . oh, never mind."

"Confidentially? I sort of wish I were going by

myself," I whispered. Then I clapped my hand over my mouth. "Sorry, I really shouldn't have said that."

"Why?" Bethel asked. "Who are you going with?"

"Ronald Rheece," I said.

Bethel's eyes widened. "Ronald? Oh yeah, that's right, Jessica told me. How did *that* happen?"

I shrugged. "I don't know. He just asked me, and, well . . ."

"Liz, that's not really an explanation," Bethel said. "Come on. You and Ronald don't exactly strike me as, um, couple material."

"We're not a couple!" I said with a laugh. "He just wanted a date for tomorrow night—"

"And you were in the wrong place at the wrong time," Bethel said. "Hey, I shouldn't give Ronald such a hard time. Even though he'll probably wear a bow tie tomorrow night, at least he had the nerve to invite you. I can't say the same for myself, you know? I found out it takes a lot of guts to invite someone to a dance. That's why I'm coming alone!" Bethel laughed, but it was kind of a sad laugh, if that makes any sense.

Just then there was a loud crash from the other end of the gym. I looked over my shoulder and saw Ronald and Blue standing by a round table that had somehow fallen over onto its side and was rolling away from them.

"I should get back," I said. "I don't know what those guys just did, but if they're alone for too long, who knows what might happen."

I hurried back to the tables we were going to be making tablecloths for. "What's going on?"

"We were moving the table, and it fell," Ronald said. "That's all."

"Ronald forgot to move his half," Blue said. "*That's* all."

I shook my head, kind of annoyed. "Well, we don't really have that much time left. Here are the markers. Who wants to draw?" I set the handful of markers on the largest table, where the tablecloths were already stacked.

"I will," Blue volunteered.

"And I'll take the finished products and place them on the tables," Ronald said.

"Sounds good." I pulled up a chair and unfolded the paper tablecloth in front of me. Blue cast me a sideways glance as he sat down next to me. I gave him a halfhearted smile and then got to work. It was very awkward, trying to draw something creative while Ronald was standing right at my shoulder, watching my every move. If it were just me and Blue, we'd probably be joking around and having a great time. And if it were just me and Ronald, things wouldn't be so bad either.

Elizabeth

Could I just ask one of them to leave? I wondered.

"So, Elizabeth, did I mention that I took a ballroom-dancing class last summer?" Ronald asked.

"Oh, um, no," I said as I drew a large sunflower.

"Yes, it was held as part of my Enriching Young Minds seminar at Sweet Valley University," Ronald went on. "The seminar tried to show us the many different ways of relating to others. One of the classic ways is through dance. For instance, we learned the rumba, the fox-trot, the waltz, the tango. . . . Let's see, were there any others?" he wondered out loud.

"How about the mashed potato?" Blue asked.

For some reason, I wasn't amused.

"That is *not* ballroom dancing," Ronald said in a snobby tone. "That is a food group."

"No, it's not!" Blue said. "It's a dance from the fifties. It goes something like this." He stood up and started to flail his arms up and down, doing the dance. He looked goofy but still cute.

Ronald sighed. "What's *your* favorite dance step, Elizabeth?" he asked as Blue slid back into his seat.

"Um, I actually don't know any all that well," I said.

"What? You must be joking," Ronald said. "I

just assumed! Well, it's not too late for us to practice, I suppose. If you come over tonight, then—"

"I'm not coming over tonight!" I snapped. "I mean—sorry. It's just that I have plans already. With my family." We were all going out for Mexican food, and I was *not* missing that to practice dancing with Ronald, who I didn't even want to dance with in the first place.

"Oh. Well, how about tomorrow morning, then?" Ronald asked.

"Dude, don't worry about it," Blue said. "Elizabeth's a rad dancer. Besides, Tanya and I are just showing up and dancing. No practice. I think that's what everyone's doing."

Ronald's eyes narrowed. I felt my own pulse pick up a few beats. What did he mean, they didn't need to practice dancing? Just how well did he know her anyway? "Who is Tanya?" Ronald asked.

"The girl I invited to the dance," Blue said.

"Oh. Well, that's wonderful," Ronald said. "I look forward to meeting her."

I don't! I said to myself. Then immediately regretted the thought. That was pretty mean.

"You know what? I see the DJ over there, setting up," Ronald said, suddenly perking up. "I'm going to go over and review his collection and make sure he plays a good rumba number. Is that all right, since you're not done yet?"

"That's fine," Blue told him, looking astonished. Was Ronald actually leaving us alone for five seconds? "Go ahead!" As soon as Ronald was gone, Blue turned to me. "What's up? You seem really upset. Or mad, maybe," he said. "What's wrong?"

"Huh?" I said. "What do you mean? Nothing's wrong." I smiled. I was being completely phony. But what was I supposed to say? I get to bring a date to the dance and you don't?

"Oh. Are you sure?" Blue scooted his chair over closer to me. He put his hand on my arm. "You're not mad at me, are you?"

"What?" It made me nervous to be sitting so close to him. "No, I'm not mad," I said.

"Well, did I do something to upset you?" Blue pressed.

Why wouldn't he give this up? He was making me feel really guilty because I knew I didn't have any reason to be mad or upset with him. I was just feeling really, really threatened by this Tanya girl. But I couldn't tell *him* that—not now. Not ever!

"No, of course you didn't do anything," I said. "I just, well, I'm actually sort of nervous. About pulling off our secret-date plan. Do you think we'll really get to dance with each other?" I asked. I wanted to let him know that was still important to me.

"Of course," Blue said. "I'll make it happen. Whether I have to cut in on Ronald's world-famous rumba or not!"

I laughed, but inside I was a bundle of nerves. So many things could go wrong tomorrow night. I didn't know if I could even go through with this.

How Elizabeth Spent Her Saturday

8:00 A.M. Watched cartoons with Steven.

9:30 A.M. Called Blue. Not home. Left message with Leaf.

10:00 A.M. Ronald called to see if dance lesson was still on.

10:05 A.M. Went for bike ride with Mom and Dad.

12:30 P.M. Got home; three messages from Ronald, zero from Blue.

1:05 P.M. Blue called. Had very awkward conversation.

1:15 P.M. Went to mall with Jessica for last-minute hair and other accessories.

2:00 P.M. Nervously sipped soda at food court while thinking about coming evening.

2:10 P.M. Bought new dress.

2:30 P.M. Returned new dress and went home.

3:00 P.M. Went upstairs and threw herself on her bed.

4:00 P.M. Ronald called to check on dress color again.

6:00 P.M. Ronald called. Steven told him Elizabeth was too busy getting ready to talk.

Elizabeth

"What time are we leaving for the dance again?" my mom asked. I was sitting at the kitchen table, leafing through the latest issue of *Fashion Frenzy*. I was looking at all the outfits I'd rather be wearing than what I had on, actually! But some of them were a little over the top—like the shirt made entirely of paper clips with the black leather mini.

I'd gotten ready at six-thirty, then fixed Jessica's hair, and now I was hoping my red dress wouldn't get too wrinkled from sitting around waiting for her to get ready. "We were supposed to leave at seven," I told my mom.

She glanced at the clock. "It's almost seven-fifteen. Are you sure it's okay if you're late?"

"Yeah, I'm sure it's fine," I said. Not that we had any choice. Jessica was still getting ready, and Damon wasn't even here yet.

"I wonder where Ronald and Damon are," my mom said, looking out the window nervously.

She was definitely more excited about this dance than I was.

"Well, actually, Mom, you know how Ronald only lives two blocks from school," I explained. "So he wants to just meet me there."

My mother poured herself a glass of sparkling water. "And is that okay with you?"

"Oh yeah. *Definitely,*" I said.

"What?" My mother looked confused.

"I mean, sure. Whatever's more convenient for him is fine with me." I smiled, then opened my compact to check my shiny red lip gloss. Jessica had helped me put on a little more makeup than usual. I was glad that my mom didn't have a problem with it.

"Liz? You're going to be nice to Ronald, right?" My mother sat across the kitchen table from me.

"What do you mean?" I asked. My mom gave me a look that meant she *knew* I knew what she meant. She and my dad knew Ronald because they knew Ronald's parents. They also knew he wasn't exactly my idea of a dream date. "Yes, Mom," I muttered halfheartedly.

Speaking of dream dates, I suddenly remembered that Salvador was supposed to be bringing the Doña with him that night. I couldn't wait to see the two of them both dressed up and dancing together! Salvador would be lucky if he could keep up with the Doña.

"I can't believe Damon is late—he's never late!" Jessica said as she rushed into the kitchen. "So? Do I look okay?" she asked me and Mom as she twirled around.

"You look fabulous," Mom said. "You both do!"

Just then the doorbell rang.

"I'll get it," our mom said. "You two, get your coats."

"I can't wait to see Ronald," Jessica whispered. "I'm going to give him *such* a hard time about not coming to pick you up."

"But I told him it was okay," I argued.

"So? He should know better," Jessica said. "And I'm going to tell him that the second I see him."

As we walked into the front foyer, I had a feeling Jessica was going to forget all about Ronald—and me—and everything else. The way Damon looked at her when he saw her and the way she looked at Damon . . .

"Hi," Damon said, his voice squeaking a little. "Sorry I'm late. You look great!" It was obvious he couldn't take his eyes off my sister.

I watched her walk over and squeeze Damon's hand as she said hello. Damon was wearing a sort of burnt red button-down shirt, a tie, and jeans. He'd put a little gel in his short, dark brown hair, and he had a black blazer on over his shirt. He looked older than usual. More distinguished or something. And really handsome.

He handed Jessica this box with a little corsage in it that she slid over her right wrist as a bracelet. It was very classic and understated. She kissed him to say thank you. They were *so* cute together. Mom even insisted on taking a picture of all of us before we went outside to the car.

I kept trying to get them to just be in one picture together—without me, the third wheel—but they wouldn't let me. I guess *everyone* could tell that I felt really uneasy about the night ahead.

"So, Liz. Where's Ronald?" Damon asked as we all got into the minivan.

"He's meeting us there," I said. "I mean, meeting me there."

"Oh. Well, I think it's really nice of you to go with him. I mean, considering you guys aren't really . . . you know." Damon cleared his throat. "Like, dating or anything."

"She's supposed to be with Blue," Jessica said. "That's who she's supposed to be going with. So we have to distract Ronald whenever we get a chance and let Liz dance with Blue. Okay, Damon?"

I felt my face turn about a hundred different shades of pink. Blue and Damon were in a band together, and they were pretty good friends. Did Jessica *have* to let Damon know how much I wanted to be with Blue?

Bethel

Should I? Or shouldn't I?

That was all I could think as I sat on the edge of my bed. My favorite CD was playing. I was in complete dance mode. I'd already taken a shower, steamed my dress, and curled my hair. I was nearly completely ready. All I had to do was take off my robe and replace it with my dress.

But was I doing that? No. And did I feel like I was going to anytime soon? Not really. I'd completely run out of momentum. It was like getting to the end of a long race and not being able to run the last twenty yards.

Not that that's ever happened to me, but I've seen it happen on TV, in the Olympics. And I was feeling like one of those runners that falls face first onto the track. Totally humiliated.

Something just didn't feel right. Everyone had said that lots of people were going to the dance by themselves. And I knew that was true. And normally I'd be perfectly fine about going by myself. But this time was different. Because I hated to go without Jameel.

This isn't like me, I thought, *to sit here and be miserable and not try to do something about it.* Okay, so maybe I was still mad at Jameel. But I couldn't stay mad forever.

I picked up the phone to call him. Even if he was at the LA Sparks game with his parents, I could at least leave a message and let him know I was thinking about him. I could at least try to clear the air before I went off to the dance. Maybe then I'd be able to have fun.

I waited three, then four rings. Then his family's answering machine picked up the call. I listened to the outgoing message that Jameel had recorded and smiled.

"Hi, Jameel," I said after the beep. "It's me. Bethel. I was just calling to say that, um, I hope you have a great time at the game tonight. Sorry I missed you. Give me a call tomorrow, okay?"

My mother knocked on the door. "Bethel, are you on the phone? I thought we were leaving soon."

I hung up the phone and got up from my bed. "I'm done, Mom. Give me five minutes and I'll be ready, okay?"

"I'll be waiting for you," my mother said

through the door. "If there's anything I can do to help, just let me know."

"Thanks, Mom," I said. *Could you drive to LA and bring Jameel back from that WNBA game?* I thought. *Because that would really help.*

But I'm not going to let my mistake get in the way of me having fun tonight, I thought as I slid my cranberry-colored dress over my head. Jessica had told me that you never knew what was going to happen at a school dance. I hoped that if she was right, then all the surprises were good ones.

Jessica

When we pulled into the school parking lot, there was a long line of cars in front of us.

"I see that I'm not the only one dropping someone off," my mom said. "It's eighth-grade-dance gridlock!"

"Can you believe we're getting here at exactly the right time?" I asked Damon. We were holding hands, and I squeezed his tightly. I couldn't believe how cute he looked in his jacket and jeans. Even though they were only blue jeans, he looked more sophisticated in them—like he was in high school.

"Fashionably late. Isn't that what it's called?" Damon asked me as he squeezed back. "You're definitely the fashionable part, and I'm the late part."

I laughed.

"Oh, but of course," Elizabeth joked in a snooty voice. "We always arrive at our parties at *least* a half hour late, isn't that correct?"

"If Jessica's involved, that's true," my mother

teased. She looked in the rearview mirror and smiled.

"Can we just get to the front of the line already?" I asked.

"I think this is kind of fun," Elizabeth said. "We get to see what everyone's wearing and who they're showing up with. Look—there's Bethel. And there's Salvador and the Doña!"

"El Salvador is bringing his grandmother?" I asked as I peered out the side window. Salvador was even wearing a suit jacket with his khaki pants, and his grandmother was wearing a gorgeous, elegant beige lace dress. "Now I've seen everything!" I said.

Talk about your odd couples. First Elizabeth and Ronald—now Salvador and the Doña? If I hadn't realized how lucky I was to be with Damon before? I *definitely* did now.

"Good news, Liz. I don't see Ronald outside waiting for you, like he's supposed to be," I told Elizabeth as we pulled ahead in line. "Maybe he's sick!"

"Jessica," my mother said. "That's not very nice."

"Sorry," I muttered.

"Anyway, Ronald's not sick. He called me at six, remember?" Elizabeth said.

"I think that was call fourteen of the day," I whispered to Damon.

"Poor Liz," Damon whispered back.

"Well, here we are." Mom stopped the car and popped open the sliding door. "Everyone out!"

"Thanks!" we all said as we climbed out of the van. Damon took my hand and helped me step down onto the pavement. He was being so sweet.

The three of us turned to head into the gym. That's when I saw Ronald, sitting on the brick wall outside the door. He stood up as we got closer. All I could think was, *Wow.* He was wearing a ruffled pale blue button-down shirt and a big black satin bow tie. He had a black blazer on, plus olive pants that were about an inch too short, plus shiny black patent-leather shoes that looked absolutely brand-new. He was carrying a box with the biggest corsage I'd ever seen in my life. Did he think he could pin an entire bouquet to Elizabeth's dress?

"Hi, Ronald!" Elizabeth waved to him.

I was wondering if she was dying inside, the way I was. She was acting perfectly nice. Which meant she was a way better person than me. I'd probably tell him to go home and change.

"Good evening, Elizabeth," Ronald said as she walked up to him. "You do realize you're tardy this evening?"

"We're *so* sorry," I snapped as I walked over to him. But seeing the pleading look on Elizabeth's face, I decided to make an effort to be nice. "But it was unavoidable. See that line of cars? The traffic on the way over was horrendous. Wasn't it?" I turned to Damon.

"Oh yeah. Total, um, gridlock," he agreed.

"Sorry," Elizabeth added.

"Well, I suppose we should affix this and then proceed inside," Ronald said. "You don't have an allergy to exotic floral arrangements, do you?"

Elizabeth smiled. "Not that I know of. It's, uh, beautiful," she said as Ronald lifted this purple-and-orange monstrosity out of the white box.

I couldn't help thinking that this was going to be the worst night of Elizabeth's life!

Elizabeth

This is going to be the worst night of *my life.* I cringed as Ronald tried to pin a gigantic purple-and-orange corsage to my red dress.

"The clerk at Betty's Floral Creations assured me this would be quite simple," Ronald said as he poked a pin into my shoulder.

I bit my lip and tried to wait patiently as he gave it another shot. I just hoped he didn't draw blood. Then again, maybe my red dress would hide it.

"Can I help?" Jessica offered as she and Damon waited beside us.

"No, thank you, Jessica." Ronald reached for another pin that was stuck into the cuff of his blazer. He stretched out his arms, flexed them, and prepared to insert another pin.

"Guys, you should just go on without us," I insisted.

"You sure?" Jessica asked, looking worried.

"Yeah, I'm sure. We'll meet you inside."

"Well, come on, Jess, let's go." Damon held out his arm, and Jessica slipped her hand through the crook of his elbow.

"See you soon," Jessica said with a pointed look at me.

"We'll be right in!" I promised her with a cheerful smile.

No! Don't go! I thought as I watched Damon and Jessica stroll into the gym without me.

Ronald came toward me with another silver stickpin. Couldn't they come up with a Velcro corsage for people like Ronald?

"Affixing a corsage clearly presents many challenges I was unaware of," Ronald commented as he stuck my skin with another pin.

"Ouch!" I cried. I was starting to feel like a test body for someone practicing acupuncture. Either that or a living voodoo doll. "Do you mind if I sort of finish doing this?" I asked Ronald.

"Well, that wouldn't be standard procedure." Ronald smiled nervously. "But be my guest. I'm sorry—maybe I should have practiced."

"No, it's okay," I assured him, telling myself to give Ronald a break. It wasn't as if he *meant* to be so clueless. The fact that this might be the first corsage he'd tried to pin on a girl was sort of cute. *I ought to be flattered,* I told myself, *not annoyed.* Even if Ronald wasn't my idea of the perfect date, at least he was trying really hard.

I finished clipping the corsage to the top-left side of my dress. "It's a little big for me," I told Ronald. "Do you mind if I adjust it a tiny bit?"

"No problem," Ronald said. "You're the expert, right?"

I was starting to think the night wouldn't be a total disaster when a red car pulled up beside us. The back door opened, and Blue got out onto the sidewalk. Then the passenger door opened, and a girl wearing a silver, spaghetti-strap top and a long, black skirt stepped out.

Tanya! I thought. *She's even prettier than Jessica said.* Her brown, curly hair was tied into a knot with two fancy sticks that had silver sparkles on them. Her skin was light brown, and her arms were perfectly toned. She even had some glitter sprinkled on her cheeks. There was a little gap between her top and her skirt, and I could see that she had a pierced belly button on her perfectly flat stomach.

Suddenly I felt like going home.

Not that there was anything wrong with my look. But hers just seemed better somehow. Probably because she was showing up with Blue—and I wasn't!

"Hi, Liz! Hi, Ronald," Blue said as he walked over to us. He sounded like he was in a really great mood. He looked pretty great himself, in black pants and a silver-blue button-down shirt. He was even wearing a tie—with a silvery blue ocean-fish pattern on it, of course. Blue loves everything that's even remotely connected to the ocean. But a tie? I didn't even think he owned any.

I smiled at him. "Hi, Blue!" I felt like putting my hand over the giant flower bouquet pinned to my dress. I don't think there is a worse color combination in the world than what I was wearing right then. But Blue didn't seem to notice or care. His face totally lit up when he saw me. It was almost as if he was surprised. Maybe he thought I was going to bail on the whole evening, like Jessica suggested.

"Elizabeth and Ronald? I'd like you to meet Tanya Papadakalis," Blue said in a very polite voice.

Tanya stepped closer to us and smiled. She had a beautiful smile. "Hey, nice to meet you." She nodded to me, then to Ronald. "Blue's told me a lot about you guys."

"The pleasure is all mine. I mean, uh, ours," Ronald said. He smiled at Tanya. "You don't attend our fine school, do you? I don't remember seeing you before."

"Right as usual, man." Blue playfully tapped him on the shoulder. "Tanya goes to the middle school. We know each other from surfing."

"Oh." Ronald shrugged. "Perhaps that's why I've never seen you before. I'm not much of a surfer." He laughed.

I laughed too. "Me either. I tried, but—"

"You did great!" Blue said. "You just need to practice more."

"I try to get out there every day," Tanya said. "It's the only way to stay on top, you know?"

"On top of the board?" Ronald asked.

Tanya and Blue both cracked up laughing. "Actually, I think she meant on top of the competition," Blue explained. "Which she usually is."

"Hey, Blue, you've *landed* on top of the competition. Remember?" Tanya asked. "Oh my God. That was so funny."

"I didn't mean to flatten him with my board," Blue said. "He just got in my way, that's all." They started to laugh even harder.

Suddenly it was really obvious to me that Blue and Tanya went back a long way. They obviously had all these stories—they had a connection.

Why did I get the feeling I wasn't Blue's secret date anymore? It seemed more like Tanya was

Blue's secret girlfriend! I couldn't help feeling very suspicious—on top of being jealous.

This little double-date scenario was really starting to wear on me, and the night hadn't even *begun* yet.

"So, you guys want to head in?" I asked.

"Sounds good." Blue reached for Tanya's hand. I watched them smile at each other, and I felt another pang of jealousy.

"Let's get going," I said. All I wanted was to be inside all of a sudden, surrounded by a million people. The night was off to a really lousy start. "The music's started, so—"

"Let's party!" Ronald cried, throwing his fist into the air. "I can't *wait* to tango."

I can, I thought as I took Ronald's arm and walked through the doors. I was never going to hear the end of it from Salvador, Anna, Jessica . . . the whole school, probably!

"So you really like dancing?" Tanya asked Ronald as she came up beside him.

"Oh yes," Ronald said. "In fact, I think of dance as a perfect metaphor for human relations."

"Really," Tanya said. "Well, then, what does a slam dance mean?"

As Ronald started a lengthy answer, Blue sidled up next to me. "I'm so psyched that we're here together," he whispered.

I didn't say anything. All I could think was: *But we're not! You're with Tanya.*

"Liz?" Blue whispered. "Our secret-date plan—it's still on, right?" he asked nervously.

"I don't know. Is it?" I replied. Because it definitely didn't seem that way to me!

Blue

What's Liz so upset about? I was standing right next to her, as close as I could get without Ronald wanting to punch me. I wanted to put my arm around her. I wanted to walk out onto the dance floor with Elizabeth and show her off to everyone. But that wasn't the plan. The plan was for her to hang out with Ronald for a while and for me to spend time with Tanya until we could find a way to sneak off and be alone on the dance floor for a few minutes.

"What do you mean, is the plan still on?" I asked Elizabeth. I was glad Tanya was such a good conversationalist. She could keep Ronald talking about his dance expertise for a few more minutes so that Elizabeth and I had time to talk. "Of course it's on!"

Elizabeth looked up at me. "Are you sure you wouldn't rather spend the entire night with Tanya?"

"What are you talking about?" Was Elizabeth actually jealous? That didn't seem like her at all!

"Nothing." She shook her head. "It's just, well, if you wanted Tanya to be your real date, why didn't you just say so?"

"I didn't! I don't! I mean, it's all part of the plan!" I couldn't believe we were actually having this conversation. "We're trying to convince Ronald that we're here as dates so that he'll give you and me a chance to be together. If he sees through the plan, we can forget about that!"

"Well, maybe we *should* just forget about it," Elizabeth said.

"What?" I asked. "Liz, what's wrong? What did I do? You know I want to be your date tonight." I was starting to get sort of angry at her. Did I have to remind her that she was the one who took a date with Ronald? If anyone had made this evening difficult, it was her.

"I thought you did," Elizabeth said. "But now I'm not so sure." She glanced at Tanya.

"We're only friends," I said. "Just like you and Ronald. Okay?" If Tanya happened to be slightly more cool than Ronald, was that my fault? But I wasn't interested in her like *that*. She was a buddy—like Brian or Salvador.

Which reminded me—I'd better go find those guys and hang out with them. Because hanging out with Tanya and Elizabeth at the same time obviously wasn't making Elizabeth happy.

"I don't know why you're so mad at me," I told Elizabeth. "I still want to be your secret date. So please save some dances for me, okay?" I squeezed her arm.

She looked at me with these really sad eyes. "Okay." She nodded. "Ronald, let's go find Jessica, like we promised." She pulled on the sleeve of Ronald's blazer and dragged him away.

Tanya came over to stand next to me. "Is everything okay with you and Liz?" she asked. "She nearly ran off just now. What is she upset about?"

I shrugged. "I don't know. I guess the plan isn't working the way she wanted."

"Well, the night just started!" Tanya said with a laugh. "How can she tell it isn't working? Besides, it'll get better once this place completely fills up. *Trust* me. Ronald won't even know where you guys are. Did you tell her I promised at least one tango with Ronald?"

"I did tell her," I said. "And I can't wait to see it." I grinned at Tanya, hoping she was right about the night improving. It was off to a very rocky start.

Bethel

"Hey, Bethel!" Anna waved to me from the dance floor as I made my way through the crowd.

"Hi!" I waved back. "Hi, Toby! Hi, Larissa!" The three of them were dancing together out on the dance floor.

I'd only gotten to school a couple of minutes earlier, but I was already really glad that I'd decided to come.

Everyone I knew was there—everyone! And they all looked like they were having a good time. All the decorations were shining in the colored lights. The DJ had a packed floor already, and the music was totally fun.

"Hi, guys!" I waved to Kristin as I passed her and Lacey Frells by one of the snack tables.

"Hey, Bethel!" they both said as they smiled at me.

I stopped to sample one of the chocolate-dipped strawberries. Some of the parents had really gotten into their food donations. The spread on the table was impressive!

"You look fantastic!" Jessica said as she rushed up to me. "I was starting to think you weren't coming."

"Well, I *did* have this moment where I wasn't sure. And that's why I'm a little late," I confessed.

"No problem. I'm just glad you're here." Jessica grinned. "Oh," she said, looking over my shoulder. "Kristin's waving me over. We're signed up to get pictures together with Damon and Brian, and I think it's our turn. Find me later, okay? We'll dance!"

"Sounds great," I told her as I picked up another strawberry. *Pictures together.* Why did Jessica have to tell me that? It made me think of Jameel and how I would love to have a picture of us together at the dance. It made me wish I hadn't been so stupid about inviting him.

Oh, well. I was here, and I was going to make the most of it. Being on my own wasn't the worst thing that could happen.

At the next snack table I watched as Ronald handed Elizabeth a cup of red punch, spilling a little onto the table. Elizabeth quickly grabbed a napkin and wrapped it around the dripping cup. She caught me watching them and gave me a friendly smile. I waved to her.

"Having fun?" someone behind me asked.

That voice sounds familiar, I thought as I turned around.

I couldn't believe my eyes. "Jameel? What are you doing here?" I asked.

"Translation—it's great to see you?" he asked hopefully.

I stared at his outfit: a crisp khaki-colored shirt, ironed black trousers, and a slim black tie. Maybe he was younger and shorter than my classmates—but he looked cuter than any of them! What's more, he was carrying a small box with a corsage inside. Was that for me?

"It is great to see you," I told him. "But I don't understand. I thought you were at the game. I thought you weren't coming. I thought . . . well, I thought you sort of hated me."

"What? Me—hate you? Not a chance," Jameel said. "But I thought you were mad at me. You wouldn't even talk to me ever since Wednesday."

"I was too embarrassed," I confessed, "after I asked you to come and you said no. But how did you get in here? When did you decide to come, and what about the Sparks game tonight?"

Jameel laughed. "One question at a time! Please!"

I folded my arms in front of me. "What's going on?"

Jameel bit his lip. "Why don't we go somewhere a little more private?" He pulled me aside so we were in a quiet corner of the gym. "Promise you won't be mad."

"Why am I going to be mad?" I asked. This sounded pretty suspicious.

"Well, first off, my friend Andy is collecting tickets, and he said he could get me in," Jameel explained. "I told him I wanted to come, and when he mentioned I could, I thought it would be a good idea to surprise you." He looked up at me. "Was it?"

"I'm not sure yet," I said. "What about the WNBA tickets? What about going to the game with your parents?"

Jameel shifted from one foot to the other. "You know, the decorating job you guys did in here is amazing. You wouldn't even know that there was PE class here yesterday."

I cleared my throat. "Ahem. The WNBA game?"

"Well, see . . . I never technically had any tickets to the game," Jameel said.

"What?" I couldn't believe it. "You *lied?* Why?"

"I don't know. It was really dumb, but I only invited you to the game because I was hoping it would make you ask me to the dance," Jameel said. "Not that I don't want to go to a Sparks game with you. But not tonight—are you crazy?"

"I think *you're* crazy," I said. "Tell me again how this plan was supposed to work?"

"I wanted you to ask me to the dance," Jameel

explained. "I couldn't ask you. And I felt totally stuck. I could tell you were too scared to ask me. Or maybe too embarrassed because I'm younger than you or something." He paused for a minute.

"I wasn't embarrassed," I said. "Well, maybe a little."

Jameel smiled. "I knew it! I could tell. So I thought I'd make you ask me. By making it impossible for you to not bring up the subject. Obviously it didn't go quite the way I'd planned." He paused, raising an eyebrow. "But I guess it all worked out okay anyway because here we are. Together." Jameel handed me the corsage. "Right?"

I couldn't believe it. Jameel sounded like he knew me better than I knew myself. And he wasn't mad at me! "So how come you're not mad at me for being too embarrassed to ask you?" I said.

"I was. But I like you too much to stay mad."

"You do? Good. Because I forgive you," I said, smirking.

"Me? What did I do?" Jameel asked.

"You lied about having tickets! And you really hurt my feelings when you said you wouldn't come with me—that day I called you?" I reminded him.

"Oh. Yeah, that wasn't too cool," Jameel admitted. "Sorry." He looked at me and shrugged. "I guess we both kind of blew it this time around. But I really like you, Bethel. I'm sorry if I ended up making things more complicated than they had to be."

"That's okay," I said as I opened the corsage box. I was a little flustered by Jameel saying how much he liked me—not that he'd ever made much of a secret of it. Could things really be going this well when an hour ago it seemed completely hopeless?

"Hey!" I laughed as I took out the delicate white rose corsage, surrounded by two cranberry-colored carnations. "How did you know this would perfectly match my dress?"

Jameel shrugged. "I know you pretty well. Haven't you realized that by now?"

"Well, now I do." I leaned over and kissed Jameel on the cheek.

Jessica was right. You could never predict what would happen at a school dance.

Jessica

"Jessica, what are you doing?" Kristin asked.

"You look like you're trying to land a plane," Lacey said in a disparaging tone.

I was waving my arms over my head while Damon went to get a drink of water. "I'm trying to distract Ronald. I'm trying to get him to dance with me instead of Liz," I said.

Lacey looked at me like I had lost my mind. "No way."

"Way," I said. "Obviously the girl needs a break!"

"Yeah, well, who wouldn't?" Lacey asked. "She really agreed to come with Ronald? Seriously? I mean, she didn't lose a bet or something?"

"No, she's just very *nice*," I told Lacey. "She's the kind of person who puts others' happiness above her own." Not that Lacey would know anything about that.

"Well, that's one of Liz's really great qualities,"

Kristin said with a concerned look at Ronald and Elizabeth. "But I wonder if she's regretting it now."

"Believe me," I said. "She is." *Poor Elizabeth,* I thought. She was trapped. Ronald was a dancing machine—a really bad one. If he kept this up, she'd have to leave the dance early due to bruised feet. She wouldn't even be able to dance with Blue, if she ever got the chance.

Where was Blue anyway? Shouldn't he be cutting in right about now?

Elizabeth

"Elizabeth, I need to visit with my computer chess club for a second. They've been waving me over for the last ten minutes. Do you want to come with me?" Ronald asked. His hair was sweaty from dancing, and it stood straight up in front.

"No, that's okay," I told him. "I'll wait here for you. All right?"

Ronald shrugged out of his blazer and draped it over a chair. "Are you sure? I don't want to desert you," he said.

"It's fine," I said. *You can desert me anytime!* My feet still hurt from Ronald stepping on them. He might have learned dance steps the summer before in his class, but he had forgotten them all by now. Unfortunately he couldn't admit that and kept insisting he was right. Five dances later I could hardly feel my toes.

I perched on a folding chair at the edge of the dance floor and prepared to sit the next one out.

I wanted my feet to recover by the time Blue and I got a chance to dance.

That was assuming we would. Right now might be a good time, but he and Tanya were standing under the basketball hoop, horsing around with a couple of Blue's friends. They were all trying to shoot paper cups through the hoop—even Tanya.

Oh, well, I thought. At least it was better than seeing them dance together.

Out on the dance floor Jessica and Damon were dancing next to Kristin and Brian, who looked awesome together as usual. Kristin had really done a great job coordinating the dance. I made a mental note to tell her that later. Anna caught my eye as she and Toby danced their way through the crowd and waved. I grinned and waved back. Anna and Toby made such a cute couple! Then there was Salvador and the Doña. They had been so busy dancing the night away, I hadn't even *talked* to Salvador yet.

And I was really happy to see Bethel dancing with Jameel—even though she'd said she was coming by herself, she sure looked like she had a date now. *Good for Bethel,* I thought. I loved seeing all my friends having such a good time.

In fact, this was probably the best dance I'd ever been to.

Except for one thing.

I wasn't having fun. At all.

So far all I'd done was drink one cup of punch, eat a couple of potato chips, and dance with Ronald. Of course that was what I'd signed on for: a date with Ronald. I just hadn't realized how upset I was going to be when I saw Blue with another girl. Maybe they were just friends, but the fact that I *wasn't* with Blue was what hurt the most. It was like I'd finally figured out how much I liked him. And then I'd blown it.

It's only one school dance, I reminded myself. *It doesn't mean that you ruined everything with Blue!*

The song ended, and I looked around the gym miserably, feeling completely lonely despite the room full of people. Then suddenly Salvador was standing right in front of me.

"Come on, Liz—dance with me." Salvador took my arm and pulled me to my feet.

"But what about your grandmother?" I asked as a fast swing tune started to boom out of the speakers.

"Please! Sofia needs her rest," Salvador said, imitating his grandmother's voice. "Besides, she's sick of me already."

"Okay, but what about Ronald?" I asked as Salvador took my hand. "I probably shouldn't—"

"Hello? Do you *see* Ronald? He's standing over

there talking to some chess girl. I think you've been officially dumped." I looked over Salvador's shoulder, hoping what he said was true, but I still couldn't see Ronald. "Come on, the song's practically over!" Salvador shouted above the music.

I laughed as he pulled me onto the dance floor. I put my left hand on Salvador's shoulder and grabbed his left hand with my right. It was really easy because we're the same height and we've danced together before—unlike me and Ronald.

Salvador and I started bopping all over the dance floor. It had been a while since I'd danced with him, but it still felt sort of natural—like we'd practiced, which I guess we had. During the dance marathon at the community center Salvador had tried to dip me during the tango. I hoped he wasn't going to try anything that wild tonight!

"This music is fantastic!" I shouted as he spun me around in a circle, and I stopped for a second, just in front of him.

"Let's show everyone how good we are!" Salvador shouted back. He winked at me and then spun me out again.

"Woo!" I cried as he twirled me around and then caught me again, wrapping one arm around my waist. I was having so much fun! Now, *this* was dancing. Salvador and I had never done this before, but it felt completely rehearsed and natural—like we were swing-dance champions!

I twirled around, and we did an elaborate sequence of twists and turns and spins all over the dance floor. When I came back into his arms, our eyes met. His were shining with excitement. He actually looked, well, really handsome. I laughed as he twirled me to the left and then to the right.

"Look!" he said, gesturing toward the side of the dance floor.

I glanced over and noticed that the floor around us had cleared out. Everyone had stopped—they were all watching me and Salvador!

"Are we really that good?" I said as he pulled me back toward him before spinning me out again.

"No—we're better!" Salvador said into my ear. We clasped each other's hands and started to step and whirl across the empty dance floor. *This* was how a school dance was supposed to be!

Jessica

"This is unbelievable!" I said to Kristin as we stood at the edge of the dance floor.

"Yeah! Who knew Sal and Liz could swing dance like that?" Kristin replied.

"No—not that. Liz is supposed to be dancing with at least one of her two dates!" I said. "Not El Salvador."

"They're friends," Kristin said. "She's probably glad he rescued her from the whole situation."

Whatever was going on, Elizabeth definitely looked happy. Happier than I'd seen her all week, actually. It was really fun watching her jump and jive all over the place. And even though Salvador could be kind of a goofball sometimes, he *was* a good dancer. It must be genetic, I decided. I'd seen his grandmother dance earlier, and she was fantastic. She'd probably given him lessons.

I grinned as Elizabeth twirled in a circle almost right in front of me. Then Salvador took her hand, and they practically floated across the floor toward the snack tables. Salvador let go of Elizabeth's hand and stepped backward.

Elizabeth turned around to grab his hand again . . . but Salvador was still gliding backward. In fact, he wasn't just gliding—he was sliding on a wet spot, straight off the dance floor!

It was like something out of a movie. The crowd parted, and Salvador went skidding right through them, directly into the snack table. He landed on the floor with a huge thud, and a table full of food crashed down all around him.

"Oh!" I cried. That looked like it really hurt! Kristin and I hurried over to Salvador along with the rest of the crowd.

Elizabeth

I watched as the Doña and Toby helped Salvador get to his feet. He couldn't walk on his ankle—he couldn't put any weight on it at all. His face was stuck in a painful grimace, and I thought I saw tears in his eyes.

"I'm so sorry!" I said as I walked up to him. A huge crowd had gathered around us.

"It's not your fault." He shook his head. "I slipped!" He bit his lip as he hopped forward on his uninjured foot.

"I'm taking him to the hospital," Salvador's grandmother said. "It'll be faster than waiting for an ambulance. Toby, could you help me take him out to the car?"

"Of course," Toby said.

Salvador looked at me again. "Well, we *were* the dance sensation of the night. You'll have to carry on without me—"

"Not a chance," I said. "I'm going to the hospital with you. Is that okay?" I asked the Doña.

"Of course," she said. "I'd love it if you came.

You can talk to Sal while I drive. Try to make him forget how bad he feels!"

"Toby and I want to go too," Anna said.

"Is there room for all of us?" I asked the Doña.

"Not really," she said. "Sal's going to need to prop his foot up and lie down on the backseat. One more person could fit in the front with Liz, but not two."

"Then I'll call my parents and ask them to pick up me and Toby," Anna said. "And we'll meet you over there as soon as we can."

"Okay—sounds good," I said. "I'll be out at the car in two seconds," I promised Salvador. "Hang in there. You're going to be okay." He looked like he was in so much pain, I could hardly stand it.

I frantically searched the crowd for the two people I needed to find. Sure enough, there was Ronald across the room, hanging out with his chess-club friends. I rushed over to him. "I'm really sorry, Ronald. I hate to do this to you," I said.

"Do what? What are you doing?" Ronald asked.

"I'm going to the hospital with Salvador," I said.

"Oh. That did look like a nasty spill. Of

course you should leave with your friend. I'll see you at school, I'm sure."

"Really?" I asked, shocked. Ronald didn't even seem to care that I was leaving. In fact, he'd already turned away to talk to someone else. What was *that* about? That's when I noticed the girl he was talking to.

"Well, as I was saying, Natalie, the Pythagorean theorem is really quite simple. . . ." Whoa. What was going on here? Natalie was staring at Ronald and smiling as if he was talking about the most interesting thing in the world. The pieces all suddenly fit together. And I wasn't happy about it. *I* was the one who was supposed to be on a secret date, and here was Ronald, hitting it off with another girl!

Then I realized how silly that last thought was, for a bunch of reasons. Number one, I didn't like Ronald like *that,* so I should just be happy that he was hanging out with a girl he obviously liked. Number two, I hadn't even had to say yes to Ronald in the first place. Maybe if I'd told him the truth, that I really wanted to go with someone else, he would've asked Natalie to go with him instead and had a much better time (not that he didn't look like he was having a good time now). And number three, *I* was the one sneaking a secret date.

"Well, good night, Ronald. I hope you enjoy the rest of the dance," I said as I patted Ronald on the shoulder. He turned to look at me again.

"Good night, Elizabeth. Thank you for everything." Suddenly I felt a huge lump of guilt rise up in my throat. *Thanks for what? For lying? For assuming you'd rather be at the dance with me than with someone who really likes you?* Wow, I had been a huge jerk. To Ronald and to someone else too.

"No, thank *you!*" I said as I rushed off to look for Blue. I didn't see him anywhere. I didn't see Tanya anywhere either. *Great,* I thought. *This is just great. I can't even—*

"Liz?" Blue grabbed my arm as I pushed my way through the crowd toward the exit. "Is Sal going to be okay?"

"I think he broke his ankle," I said. "I'm going to the hospital with him, so—I guess I'll see you later."

"No, you won't." Blue pulled me toward the door, and we rushed out into the cold night air. "Because I'm coming with you."

"But what about Tanya?" I asked.

Blue laughed. "She practically pushed me out the door when Anna told us you were leaving," he said. "Don't sweat it!"

"I'll call Mom and Dad and tell them where

you are," Jessica said as she hustled out the door after us. "And I'll call your brother too!" she promised Blue. "Let us know what happens as soon as you can!"

Blue and I sprinted to the Doña's car. This night was turning out to be a lot weirder than I'd even imagined!

Blue

"Well, that'll teach you to be the life of the party," Dr. Benson said as he slid Salvador's X ray into the lighted viewer above the hospital bed. He pointed out the fracture on Salvador's ankle. "That's a very bad break. What dance step was that, exactly?"

"I think it's called the, ow, twist," Salvador said, grimacing.

His grandmother smiled. "Even when you're lying there flat on your back, you won't stop joking, will you?"

"That's good," Dr. Benson said. "You'll need your sense of humor to wear a cast for this long."

What a weird way to end the night! Bummer! I thought as I watched Salvador lying there on the hospital bed. Every time the doctor or nurse touched his ankle, he winced in pain. They had finally given him something for the pain, and now he was waiting for them to start putting a cast on his leg.

His grandmother was holding both of his hands in hers. Elizabeth was standing right next to the bed. She kept telling Salvador different jokes, trying to get him to relax. I knew she felt bad about what had happened.

"Poor Salvador, huh?" I said to Anna and Toby, who had shown up about fifteen minutes after we got to the Sweet Valley Health Center.

"He looks awful," Anna said as she nervously chewed her thumbnail.

"Don't worry," Toby told her. "It's only his ankle. It'll heal." He wrapped his arm around her shoulders and squeezed.

"I know. I just hate hospitals," Anna said. She looked down the hallway as we heard beeping sounds coming from another room. "I hate being anywhere near the emergency room."

"It'll be okay," Toby assured her as he put his other arm around her and gathered her into a close hug.

I moved off to give them a little privacy. Anna seemed really upset, and I knew she didn't need me hanging around.

I wandered up and down the hall for a few minutes. Every once in a while a nurse or an orderly would pass me and give me a little smile. I felt really dumb, hanging around a hospital in my best clothes.

When I got back to Salvador's room, the doctor was pulling a cloth curtain around his bed. The Doña and Elizabeth were moving toward the open doorway.

"I'm going to stay here while they set his ankle," the Doña said. "Why don't you two check back in a little while?"

Elizabeth nodded. "Okay. Is there anything I can get you?"

"Well, how about a cup of coffee? If it's not too much trouble," the Doña said. "With cream."

"We'd love to get that for you," I said. I held out my hand for Elizabeth to take. She seemed pretty shaken by the whole hospital experience too. I squeezed her fingers as we started walking toward the hospital's snack-bar area, which was at the end of the hall. "Are you doing okay?"

She nodded. "Yeah. I just feel *responsible*. You know?"

"Well, look at it this way," I said. "You guys' dance was the highlight of the evening. It's all anyone will be talking about on Monday, right?"

"And Sal will definitely love all that extra attention you get when you have a cast," Elizabeth said with a wry smile. "Oh no. I can hear it now. He's going to make me get *everything* for him."

We stopped and got ourselves each a soda from the vending machine.

"So I guess nothing worked out the way we planned tonight," I said as we sat down at a small table by the window.

Elizabeth shook her head. "Not at all! I mean, I was worried about finding a couple of minutes to spend with you. Now here we are, totally alone—except we're in the middle of the hospital."

"Not exactly where I pictured spending the evening," I said. "For one thing, my shoes squeak so loud on this floor. It's really embarrassing."

"Plus everyone keeps giving us weird looks because we're so dressed up," Elizabeth said.

We looked at each other and smiled. "So are you still mad at me for bringing Tanya to the dance?" I asked.

Elizabeth took a sip of her orange soda. "Oh." She blushed a little. "I'm not mad. I guess I'm just worried. I mean, if you like Tanya, then—"

"But I don't," I insisted. "Not the way I like you. She's a friend—a buddy. I think of her as one of the guys."

"But she's beautiful," Elizabeth said.

I shrugged. "So? She's not nearly as pretty as you." I watched Elizabeth's face go from pink to red. Even under the horrible fluorescent hospital lights, she still looked good. "You know, we never got that dance," I said.

"No, we didn't," she said, finally looking up at me with a smile.

"Our whole secret-date plan? It was a flat-out failure," I said. "Let's never try that again."

"Agreed," Elizabeth said. "Hey, I have an idea. I'm going to get the Doña's coffee and bring it to her, and then I'll be right back. Wait right here for me, okay?" She jumped up from her chair and put some coins into the coffee machine.

"Okay," I said. "Where are you going? Why can't I come with you?"

"It's a secret," she said. "But I'll be right back. Here—get yourself a candy bar or something if you want." Elizabeth handed me her purse, then started striding down the hall.

What was she up to?

Elizabeth

"How is he doing?" I asked the Doña as I handed her the cup of hot coffee. "Careful—it's very full. The vending machine went kind of crazy."

"Thank you." The Doña lifted the cup to her lips and sipped. "Well, they're finishing up the cast. Salvador's a little woozy from everything they've given him. He wasn't making much sense, but he did ask me to thank you."

"Thank me? For what?" I asked.

"For the dance." The Doña smiled. "You two always look so great together. And you looked especially good on the dance floor!"

"I don't know about *that*," I said. I looked up and down the hallway. "Where did Anna and Toby go?"

"After they visited with Salvador, they went home," the Doña said.

"Oh. Well, Blue and I are down at the snack area. If my mother or father shows up in the next few minutes, will you tell them where to find us?" I asked.

"Yes, I will." The Doña sank into a blue plastic chair in the hallway outside Salvador's room. "This has been a very exhausting night!"

I knew exactly what she meant. I walked over to the nurses' station. When we'd first brought Salvador in, I'd thought I heard music playing—and not the same icky Muzak that was playing over the overhead speakers in the waiting room. Fortunately it was a really slow night at the health center. I didn't feel like I was creating too much trouble when I stopped at the desk. "Excuse me?" I said. "I have a favor to ask you."

"Yes?" The nurse behind the desk looked up at me with a bright smile. "How is your friend?"

"Okay. But I was wondering if you had a little radio back there that I could borrow for a few minutes," I said.

"You're going to cheer him up with some music?" the nurse asked. "That sounds nice."

It does sound nice, I thought. *Except that isn't my plan! Sorry, Sal. We had our dance.*

"Here you go. Just make sure you bring it back before you leave tonight." The nurse handed me the small radio. As I walked down the hall, I tuned in my favorite station. *Please let a good song be on,* I thought.

I stopped in the entryway to the vending-machine area. Fortunately we were still the only people in there. I put the radio on a table and turned it up a little. Blue turned around, surprised at the sound of the music.

"Hey. We can have that dance now," I said as I held out my hand. I could feel a huge, embarrassed grin spreading across my face. "I'm really sorry about acting so stupid earlier. And I'm sorry I didn't invite you to the dance in the first place."

"Sorry I didn't invite you fast enough," Blue replied as he stood up and gave me a hug. "Forgive me?"

"You're forgiven," I said. We started moving around the linoleum floor, dancing to the slow song, holding each other tightly. Blue's shoes were squeaking, and overhead pages for doctors kept blaring over the music, and the pins from Ronald's giant corsage were digging into my skin.

But I hardly noticed any of it. I was so happy to be dancing with Blue. His blue eyes were so pretty, even under the fluorescent lights.

"You know what? Forget school dances from now on." Blue brushed a loose strand of my hair out of my eyes. "Hospital dances are much better." He looked at me for a second with a question in his eyes, then he pulled me closer, and I felt this tingle run down the back of my neck. Finally he tilted his face toward mine and brushed my lips with his. I didn't feel nervous, or scared, or anything. I just felt happy.

"I have to agree," I said as I leaned back and smiled at him. "Hospital dances are the best."

I hoped the nurse didn't want her radio back anytime soon. I planned to stay there with Blue as long as I could.

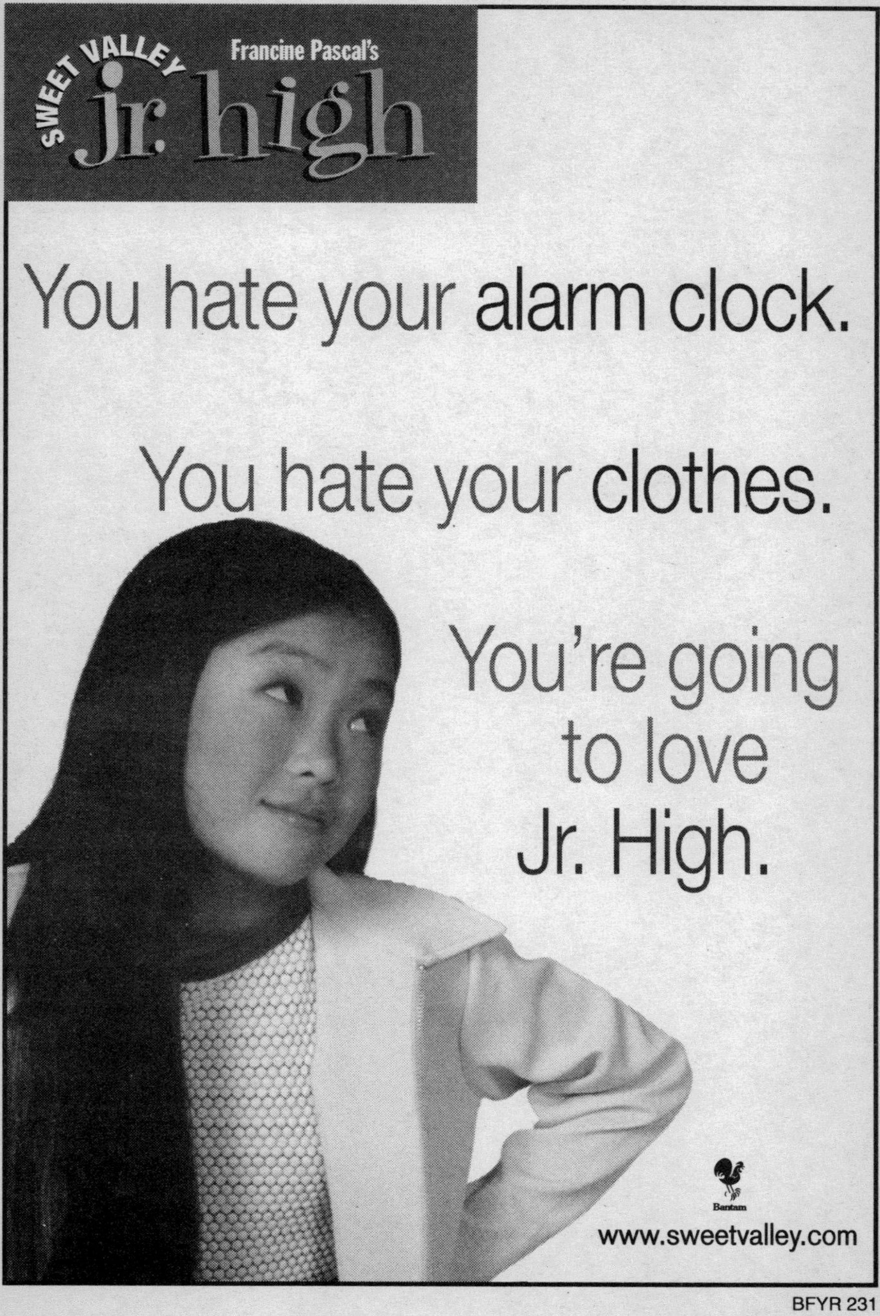
SWEET VALLEY
Francine Pascal's
jr. high
You hate your alarm clock.
You hate your clothes.
You're going
to love
Jr. High.
Bantam
www.sweetvalley.com

BFYR 231